NOT SINGING EXACTLY

NOT SINGING EXACTLY

the collected stories of
SIÂN JAMES

with an introduction by
KATIE GRAMICH

honno

Published by Honno
'Alisa Craig', Heol y Cawl, Dinas Powys
South Glamorgan, Wales, CF6 4AH

First Impression 1996

© *Siân James 1996*
Introduction © *Katie Gramich 1996*

British Library Cataloguing in Publication Data

A catalogue record for this book is available from the British Library

ISBN 1 870206 18 5

Published with the financial support of the Arts Council of Wales

Cover painting, Red self-portrait *by Shani Rhys James,*
reproduced by kind permission of the artist and of the
National Museums and Galleries of Wales

Cover design by Penni Bestic

Typeset and printed in Wales by
Gwasg Dinefwr, Llandybïe

Contents

Acknowledgements

Some of the stories in this collection were first published or broadcast elsewhere: 'Love, Lust, Life' and 'Not Singing Exactly' in the *New Welsh Review*; 'John Hedward', 'Maid in Heaven', 'Luminous and Forlorn', 'A Most Moderate Lust', 'Delia, Oh Delia', 'Free' and 'Happy as Saturday Night' on BBC Radio 4; 'The Whirligig of Time' and 'Anniversary' in *Woman's Journal* and 'The Rugby Match' in *Good Housekeeping*. Thanks are due to the editors concerned.

Introduction

> Three lovely notes he whistled, too soft to be heard
> If others sang; but others never sang
> In the great beech-wood all that May and June.
> No one saw him: I alone could hear him
> Though many listened.

Like the speaker of Edward Thomas's poem 'The Unknown Bird', the sad narrator of Siân James's title story cherishes the memory of her one afternoon of happiness, when she listened to the birds 'not singing exactly but making little happy noises.' For both writers, the bird is an emblem of freedom, representing a natural state of being from which the human is forever exiled. Characteristically, though, Thomas's speaker is engaged in an anguished quest to identify the bird and its song; this quest becomes a search also for home and self. James's character, on the other hand, is content to hold that memory in a secret part of her being; uneducated, deprived, abused, she indulges in no intellectual questioning of the birds' 'little happy noises'; she has no wish to discover the name of the species nor to make enquiries about its habitat. In the middle of her poverty and in a world where she has learnt to accept her exploitation by a brutal patriarchy, she simply clings on to her memory of the birds' voices, which become the poignant expression of her continual frustration and longing.

The title story is an apt introduction to the volume, for this is a collection of women's and girls' voices: with only one exception, all the stories have either a female narrator

or a female protagonist. Although there is a great variety of
setting and period, all these female characters are speaking of
their experiences within a male-dominated society. Many of
their experiences are bleak, as in 'Not Singing Exactly', 'A
House of One's Own' and 'Happy as Saturday Night',
where the female characters suffer sexual abuse and domestic
violence. Nevertheless, even in these horrifyingly realistic
stories, the tone is not entirely pessimistic. There is a
pleasing emphasis on female friendship, humour and
mutual support, which are so different from the roles of
rivalry and jealousy prescribed for women by the men who
wish to confine them.

Sisterhood is quite literally the focus of attention in a
number of stories, such as the memorable 'Mountain Air',
where the sisters' self-contained world of gaiety and
vibrancy contrasts with the shadowy, pinched world of their
men. Similarly, the mother-daughter relationship is given
due prominence in these stories, which are often told from
the point of view of the daughter, who tries to understand
the inscrutable adult world through interpreting and
mimicking the actions of her mother. The male tradition of
Anglo-Welsh writing has long been recognized as possessing
a special forté in child narrators, as in the work of Dylan
Thomas, Richard Llewellyn, and Leslie Norris, but Siân
James is surely asserting a distinctively female tradition in
the acutely observed girl narrators of 'Mountain Air', 'Home
Sweet Home', 'Luminous and Forlorn', 'Myra's Mother
Goes Gallivanting', 'Hester and Louise' and 'Outside
Paradise'.

More often than the overt expression of violence and
abuse, though, these stories display the disappointments
and frustrations of a boring, decent domesticity. Sometimes,
James focuses on an epiphany-like episode when years of
drudgery become transformed by a sudden passion, as in

the wonderful, Chekhovian 'Love, Lust, Life'. James is a writer who never underestimates lust; she often foregrounds a woman's sexual awakening, indicating its central importance in the assertion of a person's identity, while at the same time showing how vulnerable and powerless sexual passion can make the individual. In the single story narrated by a man, 'Anniversary', James shows that the same process can operate on the male, too – here, the unsympathetic deceiver is deceived by his wife and his lover, and is left hopeless and bereft, at which the reader, perhaps, rejoices. More often, though, it is the woman who is, in a sense, fettered to men by her own sexuality: the story 'Free', with its intensely ironic title, is an eloquent expression of the tyranny of sexual passion. Only in one story, 'A Most Moderate Lust', is the escape from such passion successfully achieved, with a rejection of 'compulsory heterosexuality' itself in favour of a more satisfying lesbian relationship, which leaves the thoroughly undeserving man out in the cold.

Nevertheless, these stories are not simply enactments of the battle between patriarch and female rebel. Female passivity and acceptance of the patriarchal order form a recurring theme. Siân James reveals clearly how male dominance is perpetuated by women like 'Delia, Oh Delia', who just puts up with her odious husband because 'he can't help being rough and nasty.' In this story Delia is infuriatingly forgiving, but at least she is making plans for beginning to live after her husband's death. Other female characters' passivity seems more hopeless; browbeaten into believing in her own inferiority, the narrator of 'Not Singing Exactly' mutely accepts a rich man's sexual exploitation as part of the deal: 'I don't even think of refusing it.'

While 'Delia, Oh Delia' has a Welsh setting, 'Not Singing Exactly' takes place in central England; despite the meticulously rendered cultural specificity of these settings, it seems that women's position in these different societies is depressingly similar. In fact, the majority of the stories have a vividly realized Welsh setting, reminiscent of many of Siân James's novels, such as the well-known *A Small Country* or the more recent *Love and War* and *Storm at Arberth*. James is so sure of her Welsh settings that she often indulges in humour and mockery, such as in the convincingly tender machinations of the Welsh parents in 'Free' or in the frustration of the adolescent protagonist of 'Luminous and Forlorn', who lives in horror of turning into 'someone in a Welsh tapestry two-piece who's into *cyd-adrodd.*' Some stories are set in London or in other specifically English locations, while James occasionally brings the Welsh to England (as in 'The Rugby Match') or the English to Wales (as in 'A House of One's Own'). Despite the possibilities for political commentary suggested by the latter, she does not seem particularly interested in politics: her cottages in Wales do not burn down, nor do her factory workers go on strike. Nevertheless, sexual politics is at the centre of this collection and, arguably, the reform of sexual politics might one day effect a revolution in the wider political sphere. The sister-hood and motherhood which are celebrated in these stories need only to become politically aware for the birds to start singing, exactly.

KATIE GRAMICH
February 1996

Love, Lust, Life

Let's face it, we'd already talked about everything else, said everything there was to say. Childhood, parents, schools, holidays, babies, children, husbands, farming, teaching; we'd been over it all several times. I knew Glyn, her husband, devoted enough he seemed in a morose sort of way, her daughter Alison, her son Huw, their young families. She was on nodding terms with my husband Russell, who looks every inch the headmaster he is and my sister Gwenda, unmarried, who works in a solicitor's office and breeds Sealyhams.

You see, we'd been together for three months, off and on. Both of us dying of cancer, but Molly going for it with more panache, swearing more, cursing more, crying more; me altogether quieter, always the lady. (Even if you saw us both in the hospital's salmon-pink dressing gowns, waiting for our X-rays, you'd know at once which of us was the farmer's wife, which the teacher.)

We were both reasonably attractive, now that our hair had grown back. Molly had a broad face and rather a wide nose, but the most beautiful lips and full breasts. I'm tall and thin with high cheek-bones and no figure to speak of.

Of course, as we're both in our fifties, talking about sex didn't come naturally to us. We'd often notice the pretty young nurses drawing together, looking naughty, having a giggle, but they were a different generation. Until that particular evening, we'd always skirted delicately round that most delicate subject. But now Molly had decided to plunge in.

'Sex,' she said, that evening, 'a strange business, isn't it? Very. There was never much of it in my marriage. Was it my fault, I wonder, or Glyn's? Of course we got married too soon, perhaps it's always too soon. I'd never been out with anyone else.

'Yes, I'd certainly fancied boys while I was at school, there was one boy in particular, oh, he was very handsome, and brilliant at games and a lovely singer as well, a nice light tenor, but of course he hardly knew of my existence.

'Glyn was older. He'd left the secondary school before I'd started there, but he started coming to the house with my brothers; he was a friend of my brothers. That's how I got to know him.

'I didn't know anyone else. We lived on a smallish farm a couple of miles outside the village, six miles from town, who was there for me to get to know? There was no one in the chapel we went to. Occasionally some traveller in animal feed would call and chat me up over a cup of tea in the kitchen, but it never came to anything. My father or my brothers would see to that. So I used to look forward to Glyn coming on a Saturday. Not that he came to see me. He had an old Morris van and he'd come to call for my brothers and they'd go to the pub for the evening, but when he brought them back he'd come in and stay for half an hour or so and I used to look forward to those times. He'd have a cup of coffee or some home-made wine and after a while he'd mellow and put his arm around me and I'd fling it away and he'd laugh and my brothers would laugh and that's how it would go on.

'Ours was a poor farm, since my mother's death, anyway. It was more comfortable while she was alive. She did a lot of cooking and cleaning and always kept a good fire in the grate. Not that it was anything like the Archers' farm at Ambridge even then, perhaps Welsh farms never are. Anyway it wasn't so bleak then – when she was alive, I mean. Spring was always a celebration, somehow. Not Easter or the religious festival – though she did go to chapel and believed in all that – but just the breaking of the earth's crust, lighter mornings, the first blossom on the blackthorn. There was always a renewal of hope then. My mother died of cancer. Well, it's a popular illness, isn't it? Yes, she'd be in her early fifties, too.

'Anyway, to get back to Glyn. Idris, the older of my brothers, told me that he was serious about me and wanted to take me home to meet his parents the next Sunday. "Get yourself a new dress," Idris said. And he gave me a ten pound note. Bloody hell, I knew it was serious, then. Ten pounds was a fortune in those days. I'd never even held a ten pound note before.

' "I don't really know him," I said. "I don't know whether I like him." "You can find out, can't you," Idris said. "Yes, but if I take this money, that'll be it, won't it?"

' "We like him. Dad likes him. He's a solid chap. They've got a really good farm, the Morrises, much bigger than ours, with a lot of modern outbuildings and modern machinery. You'd be a fool to let him go, there's plenty of girls who'd have him. And besides, Alun is wanting to get married and it would be easier for him to bring Beatrice here if you went."

' "Beatrice Williams? I didn't know there was anything in that."

' "Yes," Idris said, "and a bit more than anything, too. Well, I know she's a bit older than him, but she's a big girl and she'd make something of this place. She'd have more interest, wouldn't she? You've never had the interest. That's natural. We don't blame you."

' "What about you, then? Aren't you going to get married?"

' "I wouldn't have to, would I? Not if Alun does. I'd be in

charge of the farm, that would be enough for me. And if Beatrice has two or three little ones – to be absolutely honest there's one on the way now – that would be as many as we'd want, wouldn't it? As many as we've got room for. Anyway, that's the position. Have a think about it. No hurry mind. Only get that dress, in case you decide on it come Sunday."

'Beatrice Williams in the family way and our Alun the father. That's all I could think of that night in bed. But she was old, at least ten years older than Alun, about fifteen years older than me, well into her thirties.

'Idris and Alun were very close, always had been, and neither of them was close to me, but all the same, it was strange that I'd heard next to nothing about Alun and Beatrice. How long had they been courting? I couldn't imagine them making love. Where had they done it? He never brought her to our house. Outside in the fields? Or in her widowed mother's bungalow after she'd gone to bed? I thought about them much more than I did about Glyn and me. I tried – and failed – to connect them with all the things I'd read in magazine stories, Mills and Boon and school books like *Wuthering Heights*. In a decent suit Alun, though a few inches on the short side, wouldn't be altogether deficient, particularly if he shaved off his sideburns, but Beatrice Williams had frizzy black hair and little round eyes like currants and she weighed about fifteen stone.

'I suppose you could say that I got married to make room for fifteen-stone Beatrice Williams. I deserved all I got, didn't I?

'Anyway, it could have been worse. Glyn's parents were decent enough and they liked me well enough, I think.

'After I'd been there to tea in my new dress and jacket – French navy, not too bridal – Glyn became my official sweetheart, and that winter started staying for the night every Saturday after being to the pub with Idris and Alun, unofficial that part, and we got married in early spring.

'Beatrice, married to Alun by this time, was already living with us, and I must say she was a startling worker and cheerful and affectionate too, making a big fuss of me on my wedding day and a big fuss of Alun every day. She was a good girl and there's no doubt that she pulled the farm together. And she certainly kept Alun happy.

'Glyn's parents expected me to work hard, but there you are, they worked equally hard themselves and they were very easy with money, fair play to them.

'I suppose the marriage turned out quite well on the whole, plenty of hard work, but I was used to hard work, and better conditions than I'd known before and more money for little luxuries. Glyn wasn't as silent and dour in those early days, before his father died leaving him all the responsibility. I had Alison the next year and Huw Meredydd the following one and then I went on the Pill. And after that we had a few years of illness and death, my father, Glyn's father, Glyn's mother; the black years, with even more work for me nursing as well as everything else.

'And all this time, sex had been the least important thing. Just a strangely primitive rite that happened once a week or so, accompanied by a lot of grunting and sweating on Glyn's part and not much more than silent acceptance on mine. Once or twice when he bothered to kiss me first, or chatted and laughed with me, I got some hint of how it seemed to be in books, but nothing in me ever glowed or bloomed or sang, never mind exploded.'

Molly was silent for a while, lying back quite still on her pillows. Her face was rather flushed. For a moment I wondered about ringing for the nurse. When she next spoke her voice was quite different, low and tender, as it was when she was talking to her youngest grandchild.

'I'm going back twenty years now,' she said, 'back to the time I was about thirty-two or three. The children were at secondary school and we were comfortably off. Glyn was never as free with money as his parents had been, but I had a bed and breakfast business by this time, which was giving me financial independence – I'd even got myself a small car – as well as pleasure and a bit of company.

'Glyn never wanted to spend money on the house, but I'd soon got a bit saved and one year decided on having a second bathroom and the next year, to convert the attic into two small bedrooms for the children so that I could take over their bigger rooms for more visitors. I hated having to turn down bookings.'

Another silence, shorter this time.

'Well, this is it now. My spring awakening. Was it spring? Yes, early spring, February perhaps. Definitely before the Easter influx of B&Bs. His name was Mike Taylor. He was the builder who came to give us the estimate for the work I wanted doing. Glyn had met him in a pub in town, the landlord had put in a good word for him and Glyn had asked him to call the following week.

'He came early on the Monday morning. He was there by the front door when I got back from taking the children to the bus-stop in the village. "I'll get my husband," I said. "Come in and wait in the kitchen."

'Even in the first minutes I was aware of him, nervous of him, my mouth dry. He was about twenty-eight, tall, with very blue eyes in a thin, dark face. An arrogant face and an arrogant way of leaning against the porch and then following me silently into the house.

' "What the hell do you need me for?" Glyn asked, annoyed that I was expecting him to leave his work in the yard. "It's you that wants the bloody thing altered."

' "Yes, but he'll take more notice of you. He's that sort."

'So Glyn took his boots off and we went upstairs and Glyn told him what we wanted done. "And I'll be getting another estimate," he said, "if I think you're charging too much."

' "Bloody farmers always think they're being overcharged," Mike said. "I'll give you my price and then you can tell me to fuck off. You'll enjoy that."

' "And don't swear in front of my wife," Glyn said.

'Mike glanced up at me with a sort of quiet insolence. "I'll get on with the measuring," he said.

'Glyn and I went downstairs. "I don't like him," I said. "I think I'll decide on old Sam Miles after all."

' "I'm not having that waster here. He's drunk oftener than he's sober. This chap will do the work in half the time."

' "I don't like him," I said again.

'Anyway, the estimate he sent us was reasonable enough and as he could start work the following week, I let Glyn ring up to accept it.

'I felt nervous again as I took him upstairs the next week. The attic had one small window. I remember looking out from it at the field where Glyn was ploughing and then back at him, where he was taking measurements for a Velux window we were having in the roof.

'And as though he could feel me looking at him, he turned to look at me. For a long time he looked; a long, silent appraisal.

' "Open your blouse," he said then.

' "What? What did you say?"

' "Open your blouse."

' "How dare you! Who do you think I am?" I felt myself shake with anger.

' "You followed me up here. So let's see what you've got on offer. Open your blouse."

'It was such a shock that I burst out crying. You see, he was right. I had followed him up to the loft. He knew his way perfectly well, knew exactly what he had to do. Why had I gone up with him? Only because he was so full of . . . well, of something that I obviously wanted, I was shocked and ashamed how much. And now that I'd started, I couldn't seem to stop crying. It wasn't anger now, but shame and grief. And something else I could hardly name as it was such a new, such a new and overwhelming sensation.

'"Never mind, never mind," he was suddenly saying, his arms tightly around me. "I didn't mean it, I promise. Only I'm a direct sort of chap and I always think other people are the same. You see, I fancied you last week and I thought you fancied me. You did too, didn't you? You see, I could tell. But all right, you don't want to do anything about it. Well, it's up to you. It's your decision. Perhaps you've got used to a bit more style than I've got. You dry your eyes now and forget all about it. Right?"

'"Right." But he was still holding me very closely. Almost as though I was a child. But I wasn't a child, but a woman with a pain, a pain like hunger.

'"So you go downstairs and forget about this, all right?"

'"All right." Everything was all right as long as he went on holding me. By this time he'd opened my blouse and was stroking my breasts so tenderly and sweetly that I couldn't bear to break away from him. When I tried to move, it was like trying to move in a dream. I couldn't move.

'"Right. So now you go straight downstairs and forget all about this. OK? Oh, but what beautiful breasts you've got, what beautiful dark nipples. Can't I just kiss and so on for a minute or so before you go? Yes? Just say yes if you mean yes, because I don't want to upset you again. Yes?"

' "Yes."

' "Yes. Just for a minute or two, then. Oh, what a lovely body you've got. What a wonderful soft belly. What a beautiful curve. It's like the curve of the sky. Oh, and now I can feel the top of your sweet bush, such a . . ."

' "Stop it. Oh, stop it."

' "We can't stop now, can we? Can we? Do you think we can? You really want to stop? Listen, just kiss me then. We can kiss, can't we, before you go downstairs? Don't be afraid to kiss. Properly. That's right. Suck my tongue tight into your mouth. That's right. Oh, do it again. Again."

'Oh, it was shameless and wonderful, that kiss, which went on for ever, stirring every cell in my body to quivering, trembling life. How could I forget that kiss and what came after? I couldn't. Even if I was a Christian and hoped for eternal life, I couldn't renounce the memory of it or deny that it was the greatest, most wonderful experience of my life, because that was the time I came alive as a woman. That's when I came alive, crying and wet as a new-born baby, but a grown woman and a different woman.

'And every day afterwards, all the time he worked for us and later, I made love with him, had sex, committed adultery, sinned, sinned, with the same joyful and shattering abandon, relishing every new and extraordinary and undreamed-of thing we did together, he leading and pleading and petting and praising and me following, obeying, wanting everything. And then wanting it again.

'You'd think I'd have forgotten it now, wouldn't you. All that fever and passion. All so long ago. You'd think I'd want to forget it. All the intrigue and lies, the interrupted phone calls and the hurried, famished meetings. You'd think that after he left me, because of course he did, he did leave me, though not until he'd got married himself almost five years later and left the area. Still, you'd think I'd want

to put it firmly behind me by this time. You'd think I'd
want to spend my last weeks, or last days, thinking of
higher things, wouldn't you? So many lovely things to
remember. The rush of spring, the quiet of a summer
evening, trees in autumn, trees, trees, mountains, snow on
the mountains. All those lovely things. And babies. My
own, Beatrice and Alun's little ones, my grandchildren, this
new one, this new little life. But that . . . you know . . . that
was the best of all. The best.

'Well, I wanted to say that, wanted to tell someone about
it. My breasts and my thighs are aching just to think of it
again. Love, lust, life. I don't know which it was.

'It'll be your turn tomorrow, Jane, won't it? And I bet
you've had your moments, too, for all you look as though
butter wouldn't melt. Your turn tomorrow.'

Molly died that night. So I didn't have to tell her, after all,
of my sexual experiences. Anyway, they'd have been a
dismal disappointment; one or two tentative pre-marital
affairs and an uneventful, rather dull marriage.

I felt happy for Molly, though. And when Glyn and
Alison and Huw Meredydd came to see me after the
funeral, I was able to tell them: she had a good life. She told
me she'd had a good life.

If I cried it was for myself.

John Hedward

'Julia and Claire have each other,' the members of Appleyard told one another, 'they're very close and they were never close to Ben. After all he was only four.'

'Ben was a loner,' Deirdre Macabe said. 'He was the same age as Patsy, but he never played with her. He certainly didn't like girls.'

They all thought about Ben who was dead; dark, stocky, unsmiling.

'He had this imaginary friend,' Eric Smith said then. 'He didn't need anybody else.'

Eric seemed more reconciled to the little boy's death than the rest of them. Yet he had been fondest of him. The only one with no children of his own, he had lavished time and attention on Ben.

'John Hedward,' Eric continued, taking his pipe out of his mouth again. 'That's what he called him, his little mate. Hedward. Most particular about the 'h'. Quite a lad. Red-haired. Could climb any tree in the world. Frightened of the dark, though. And thunderstorms. When the inspector asked us why Ben had gone all that way on his own, I nearly told him about John Hedward.'

'I'm glad you didn't,' Tim Austin said, rather shortly. He worried about Eric. He wasn't quite one of them. Older for one thing. The only one of working-class origins. Not that that made any difference of course.

'The thing is,' Sheila Armstrong said in her quietly forceful way, 'the thing is, Ben is dead. We've just got to accept it. We can't do anything for Ben. All we can do now is to take special care of Julia and Claire. After all, poor Barbara is beyond anything.'

They all sighed their agreement. Poor Barbara was definitely beyond anything. The children's father had come down from London for the funeral, but his presence had been no help. The little girls hardly remembered him and Barbara had thanked him for coming as though he were a complete stranger, seeming openly relieved when he went. She'd gone back then to her large dark canvases, standing in front of them as though they held all the answers, refusing to talk. She was certainly beyond taking any notice of her daughters.

Not that she had ever taken much notice of any of her children, Deirdre thought, conscious and a little ashamed of her disloyalty.

Deirdre knew that she was different from the others at Appleyard and it troubled her. They gloried in all the tough outdoor work – they lived on their market garden – as much as their painting, sculpture and pottery. They made their own bread, wine, butter, cheese. The children too had their own tasks and were expected to create their own pleasures. They believed that a conscious determination on simplicity would result in harmony and serenity.

But Deirdre often longed for a small centrally-heated house near some shops and a nice park, Patrick coming home from his office at six o'clock, the girls in their dressing-gowns, and fish fingers for tea. Less creative than the others, she found herself with most of the household chores. How easy it would be to clean a small semi-detached house, hoover its bright carpets. The vast Appleyard rooms with their flagstone floors and draughts were beginning to get her down.

She caught her husband looking at her and tried to smile. She must strive to be like the others, she knew that. Like poor Barbara, for instance, who was really the most dedicated of them all, certainly the most gifted. They could surely bear her temporary withdrawal, Deirdre told herself, without feeling bitter about it.

As soon as the meeting was over, she went straight up to see Julia and Claire. 'Good night, little ones,' she said, giving them each a hug and a kiss. They were surprised, but not unduly discomfited. Deirdre was accepted as rather wet, but her soda scones made up for it.

With so many substitute parents anxious about them Julia and Claire hardly noticed their mother's neglect.

In school, too, everyone was especially kind to them, friends – and even enemies – bringing them sweets and comics, and their class teacher inviting them home to tea.

On the day of the funeral, the headmistress had called them in to her room to give them one of her little talks.

'At the moment, you would probably like to forget all about your dear little brother,' the headmistress had said, 'his sweet ways, because remembering him is inseparable from the pain of losing him. But I'm going to ask you to make every effort to remember him, to make friends with the pain, so that his memory will remain with you to enrich the precious fabric of your childhood. Now, will you promise me to try?'

Both little girls had nodded their heads vigorously, Claire's fractional delay being only to make sure of Julia's reaction. 'Poor, brave little girls,' the headmistress had said.

And then in her normal brisk voice, 'And now you can spend the rest of the morning sorting out the P.E. equipment for me. You'd like that, wouldn't you?' They'd nodded their heads again, even more vigorously.

And ever afterwards to Claire, who was only just seven,

the memory of Ben's death, which was to enrich the precious fabric of her childhood, was irretrievably mingled with the dusty smell of the plimsolls, bean bags, ropes and team bands which she and Julia had so carefully and tidily arranged in their different cardboard boxes on that morning after his funeral.

Only in bed at night did they ever talk about their dead brother. They worried, then, because they didn't miss him as much as they felt they should. Claire, in particular, felt very guilty, she knew she'd been far more upset when Donald, the old sheep-dog, had died.

'Anyway, I cried at the funeral,' she told Julia one hot August evening when she couldn't sleep.

'No you didn't. You just sniffed. I was watching you. Patsy cried all the time without even trying. Her face was all red and blotchy.'

'That was because she wasn't allowed to go to the funeral. She thought there was going to be balloons like we had for the Fête. That's why Patsy cried.'

'Ben didn't like us, that was the trouble,' Julia burst out. 'He didn't like us a bit.'

'He didn't really like anyone except John Hedward.' Claire sighed deeply. 'Julia, I want to ask you something.'

'He liked Eric,' Julia said, 'because he let him have matches.'

'And use the hatchet. Deirdre spoke to him about that over and over, I heard her. But Eric never took any notice. That's why he liked Eric. Because he never refused him anything. Mummy said he wasn't to have a pocket-knife, even Marcus hasn't got a pocket-knife and he's nearly six.'

'If only he'd liked us just a bit. Patsy can't wait for us to come home from school. Deirdre says she's at the gate half an hour early sometimes.'

'Patsy lets me bath her,' Claire said, 'and read to her at bedtime. She thinks I'm a very good reader.'

'Well you're not.'

'Patsy thinks I am. I read and read to her. Whole books. Ben never wanted me to read to him.'

'He used to shout if I went near him.'

'I went to his room once when he was having a nasty dream and he just said, "Go away, Nit".'

'He used to call me Fatface. Once he called me Bum.' It pained Julia to remember.

Claire wrapped a piece of blanket round and round the fingers of her left hand. There was something she longed to ask Julia, but somehow didn't dare. She sighed hugely again.

Julia settled herself to sleep, but Claire still felt hot and restless. After counting to a hundred very slowly and reciting the three-times-table until she got stuck, she wondered if a prayer would help her. Mrs Bowles, the headmistress, and Miss Denman seemed sure that prayer helped everyone, but at Appleyard no one seemed convinced. Deirdre said it helped those it helped, Eric thought it was whistling in the dark, the others seemed upset about the subject. Like Miss Denman was when she had told her about Belinda being on heat and rolling about and calling for a mate. 'It's not a suitable item for your news book,' Miss Denman had said. You could never be sure what grown-ups would get fussed about. Life was very strange and very difficult. And it seemed to be getting worse. Ben's death, even though she couldn't pretend that she really and truly missed him, as she'd missed Donald the old sheep-dog, had certainly made her very uneasy.

'I feel outside myself,' she had told Julia the previous evening. 'I've never been outside myself before. And sometimes I don't seem to remember who I am inside. I mean, who I'm outside of.'

'Don't be silly,' Julia had said.

'Gentle Jesus come,' Claire said softly,
'Through the clouds of grace.
We would be exceeding glad,
To see Thy beauteous face.'

It was her favourite prayer. Julia had made it up for a class assembly the previous year and Miss Denman had given her three stars for it. Julia was always getting stars. Her name on the merit board had three whole rows of stars after it, which was three times fifteen. Claire tried to work out that sum in her head but failed; three fives are twelve, but which figure did she put down and which did she carry and what did she do then? Perhaps she could manage it if she had paper and a pencil. Claire didn't have many stars. Only five times one. Sometimes she started a lesson, a number lesson perhaps, really determined to finish the exercise right through. But after a few sums she always felt very tired. It just got too boring. Joined-up writing was too boring as well. She didn't like doing the letters in the same way all the time, and she didn't think the letters liked it either. As soon as she put down a big R, for instance, it seemed to be begging her for loops and tails, and little o's seemed to want dots in the middle, or eyes, and then Miss Denman would say, 'Oh Claire,' and Julia and her best friend, Amanda Walters, would turn round and frown at her.

She said the prayer again. The part she liked best of all was 'clouds of grace,' though she wasn't absolutely sure what they were; grey clouds perhaps, but tinged with feathery streaks of palest rose pink.

Having pictured such clouds very vividly, she wasn't altogether sure whether she would be exceeding glad to see a face, even a beauteous face, looking through them. Wouldn't it be a bit spooky?

The unease she felt turned to a hard, gripping fear. 'Are you asleep?' she asked Julia. Her voice trembled like a voice left out in the cold.

Julia was fast asleep. The light from the landing shone in from the half-open door. Claire got up on one elbow to draw what comfort she could from her sister's nearness. She was beautiful as a princess. Even asleep she looked calm and rather disdainful. Julia would know the answer.

She leaned over towards her. 'What's happened to John Hedward?' she asked her sleeping sister. 'Oh Julia, have you thought about John Hedward?'

She felt a little better even to have voiced the question. 'Julia, Julia,' she said very loudly, 'oh please, Julia, can I come into your bed?'

Julia woke just enough to say no.

There was complete silence in the room. No sound from any of the other children in their bedrooms, no sound from any of the grown-ups downstairs. No music from anywhere, no sawing or hammering, no friendly water gurgling in the pipes. No sound.

'All right,' Claire said at last, very, very softly. 'All right John Hedward, you can come in with me. That's it, you can come into my bed. That's a good little boy. You'll be warm in a minute. Are you comfortable? You want my teddy to hold? Here you are then. I'm too old for it now, you can have it. Good night, John Hedward, sleep tight. You shall be my little friend from now on.'

Hester and Louise

When I was a girl, women looked their age, particularly if they were widows. My grandmother could only have been in her early sixties when I remember her, but she had settled comfortably into old age; wiry grey hair scraped back into a tight bun, round cheeks reddened by sun and broken veins, dark shapeless clothes, grey woollen stockings baggy round the ankles.

She'd once been a district nurse. On the mantelpiece in the parlour, there was a photograph of her standing importantly at someone's front door, large bag in hand, round hat pulled down to the eyebrows, but I found it difficult to believe in this starched image, could only see the untidy old woman she'd become; shooing the hens away from the back door with a dirty tea cloth, bending to cut a lettuce in the garden, her large bottom in the air, or her most typical pose, standing at the gate, squinting into the sun, her big heavy breasts supported on her folded arms.

I stayed with her for five or six weeks every summer, not for her benefit or for mine, but because it eased the pressure on my parents who kept a dairy in St John's Wood.

I liked London far better than the Welsh countryside. I missed the Friday evening dancing class, the Saturday morning cinema, the big public library which was only two streets away and my friends, Jennifer and Mandy.

There was no dancing class, cinema or library in Brynawel and the village children scorned me. The much praised fresh air always seemed to have an overlay of cows' shit; I much preferred stale air with petrol fumes.

I didn't like Gran's meals either; runny boiled eggs with orange yolks for breakfast, dirty looking potatoes, greens and grey meat for dinner, rough brown bread with cheese and salad for supper, with the occasional addition of caterpillar or little black flies.

I didn't like my bedroom although it had once been my father's; the bed was hard, the pillows lumpy and the sheets coarse. But worst of all, my grandmother had no bathroom and expected me to strip-wash in the back kitchen with carbolic soap and the same wet towel she'd used. The summer when I was twelve, she promised to keep out when I was washing, but twice she forgot and came barging in and once the coalman came to the door and saw me in vest and knickers. 'Oh, the man will never be the same again,' was all she said when I complained.

When I was thirteen, I begged my parents to let me stay home; pleaded and cried, promising to serve in the shop, wash dishes, even peel potatoes. 'I'll do anything, anything, but please don't send me away to Gran's.'

My father thought I was mad. He and his brother Bob had had an idyllic childhood, he said; all the freedom of the fields and woods, fishing, ratting, scrumping apples, helping the farmers with the harvest, earning sixpence a day. 'This one's a girl though, Isaac,' my mother said. 'She likes different sorts of things, girls' things, going round Woolworths and Boots and the market, buying shampoo, trying on lipsticks, things like that. Try to understand.'

'It's not just those things,' I said, since he was looking at me as though he'd never seen me before. 'It's just that Gran doesn't have a bathroom, so I don't have any privacy. And I'm not a child any more. I have my periods now and I have to wear a bra. And I'm not going to bath in a back kitchen and you shouldn't expect me to.'

That shut him up. He could never tolerate any talk of

bodily functions. And my mother promised to write a polite letter to Gran, explaining how I felt.

We had a letter back by return of post.

She quite understood the position. I was going through a little phase, that was all, and they were not to worry. She'd spoken to Hester and Louise, the Arwel sisters, though, and I was most welcome to use their bathroom any time I wanted to, twice a day if I'd a mind. And they, as I probably remembered, had an all-pink bathroom the size of a small ballroom with bottles of this and that and loofahs and sponges and a special brush for scrubbing your back, pale grey carpet on the floor and a little fluffy cover on the W.C.

'The Arwel sisters,' my father said, casting his eyes to the ceiling.

'I'll go,' I said. 'I love Miss Hester and Miss Louise. The Sundays they invite me to their house after church are the only days I enjoy.'

'She's a girl, Isaac,' my mother said again. 'Try to understand.'

Miss Hester and Miss Louise didn't seem to belong in Brynawel, but to a world I knew only from the cinema. I'd often try to describe them to my friends, Jennifer and Mandy. 'No, they're not really young, perhaps thirty-five or so, even forty, and they're like ladies in old-fashioned films with tiny waists and delicate faces like flowers. Well, I think they may have had sweethearts once, but perhaps they were killed in the war. No, they're definitely not spinsters, spinsters are altogether different. No, they don't have jobs, they just have money, plenty of money, so they can do whatever they want to. Sometimes they hire a car to take them out shopping or to the seaside or to church on Sunday. Otherwise they stay at home doing tapestry, reading magazines and changing their clothes. Oh, they're very gentle and kind. Just think of me going there each day! And I know they'll give me home-made lemonade and iced biscuits every time. I'm really looking forward to staying with Gran this year.'

The sisters called on the very afternoon I arrived, to remind me of their promise. 'Isn't she pretty,' one said, smoothing down my rough curly hair. 'Isn't she pretty,' the other replied. They always repeated each other's pronouncements. 'Hasn't she grown tall and slender.' 'Hasn't she grown tall and slender.'

'Don't turn her head,' Gran said. 'She's foolish enough already.'

'We've heard different. We've heard that she had an excellent end of term report and that she's a marvellous little pianist.'

'A marvellous little pianist, as well.'

'We want her to play for us. We've had our piano tuned.'

'We've had our old piano tuned specially.'

I'd forgotten the way they so often stood with their arms clasped tightly round each other's waists, as though they wanted to be one person instead of two.

They were dressed that day in cream high-necked blouses, full dark green skirts, black belts pulled tight and cream high-heeled shoes. They always dressed identically, though they weren't twins. Hester was a year and a half older and she was also a little taller and perhaps a little more elegant. Louise's eyes were a brighter blue, though, and her lips were fuller. I could never decide which was the more beautiful.

'Well, I must ask you to go now,' Gran said, 'because I always listen to my serial at four o'clock. I'll send the girl round after supper.'

I could never understand how Gran had the nerve to treat them so casually, even rudely, when she was ugly and poor and they were so beautiful and so rich.

'Who told them about my report?' I asked her when they'd left.

'I did, of course. I told them you were going to college to be a teacher. In case they have any ideas of turning you into a lady's maid.'

'Are they so rich?'

'Oh yes. Their father had the best farm in the county, but when he knew he was dying and with no son and heir, he had to sell it all, land and livestock, to buy an annuity for those two. Their mother had died, you see, when they were toddlers; soon after Louise was born, and he spoiled them, of course, and everybody spoiled them. Even when they were schoolgirls, they never had to do a hand's turn for themselves, let alone anything in the house or the farm. It was hard on him in the end. But what could he expect? He'd brought them up to be butterflies.'

'Why didn't they get married?'

'No one from round here was stupid enough to ask them, I suppose. To tell you the truth, your uncle Bob seemed to be thick with them at one time, but he never seemed to know which one of them he liked best and then he was called up and met your auntie Dilys, so he lost them both.

'He was a born farmer, Bob was, ready to do a day and a half's work every day. Their father would have been proud to have him as a son-in-law, and he would have been the making of those girls, but which one of them?'

'But which one of them?'

'God help us, if you're going to start being an echo like those two.'

'God help us,' I began. But she cuffed me on the head and turned the wireless on.

To think that one of them could have been my auntie. My auntie Dilys was nice enough, but she wasn't special in any way.

If I hurried over my supper and the washing up, I had two whole hours to spend at Arwel and I savoured every moment.

I'd be shown first into the drawing-room where we'd have coffee, real coffee, served in a silver coffee pot, where I sat in a fat velvet chair and was passed a cup and saucer of green and gold eggshell china, pink crystals of sugar and exotic dark chocolates. After this delightful ritual, I might look at their photograph albums; two plump little girls sitting together on a garden seat, chubby legs and solemn round faces, two young girls in frilly party dresses with ribbons in their hair, two young ladies in their first ball gowns.

'This one is you, isn't it Hester?' I'd ask.

'Wait a minute, now. I really can't tell. No one seemed sure, even at the time. They always called us the girls or the sisters, you know, never our names. We hardly knew ourselves which of us was which, did we Louise?'

'We hardly knew ourselves, did we, Hester?'

The house was so beautiful, so wickedly luxurious; thick carpets everywhere and floor-length velvet curtains, heavy as the falling darkness outside. They lent me a dressing-gown of plum-coloured chenille and after I'd bathed and washed my hair, they'd take me to their bedroom and take it in turn to brush my hair, brushing gently, gently, almost as though they were in a trance. They each had an ivory hairbrush, I remember, one with a silver H on its back, the other an L. I wished my hair was long and straight and raven-black instead of short and reddish-brown. Gran had forbidden me to use make-up, but they insisted that complexion milk didn't count, so they smoothed it into my face and my neck and my shoulders. It felt soft and silky and smelt of little white roses and purple violets, so different from Gran's carbolic soap. 'She's got such delicate skin, hasn't she Hester?' 'Her skin is as soft as a baby's, isn't it, Louise?' Afterwards I was encouraged to try on their perfumes – luckily Gran had lost her sense of smell – and I loved repeating their grand French names; *Je Reviens, Bal de Nuit, Ma Griffe, L'Air du Temps, Mon Désir, Arpège.*

Their house had several bedrooms, six or seven I should think, but they slept together in the largest and grandest one in the front. (The long small room at the back of the house was where their maid, housekeeper, cook slept, a bustling little woman called Gwladys who had been with them since their birth. They always got her to walk home with me, but she never came very far because she was frightened of the dark and I wasn't.)

They slept in a high, old-fashioned bed with a brass bedstead. The quilt was a bright turquoise silk, the colour matching the tiny rosebuds on the cream wallpaper, and the carpets, the heavy curtains and the satin lampshades were a deep, voluptuous pink. There was a highly polished bedside table on either side of the wide bed with a framed photograph on each.

One evening Hester picked up the photograph from her side, gazing at it as though willing me to notice it. I didn't need much prompting. 'What a handsome man,' I said. He was handsome; dark curly hair, slanting eyes, straight nose and full, curved lips. And as I might have guessed, Louise then brought me the photograph from her bedside, and at first I thought it was the same man in a different pose.

'Brothers,' I said then. 'Twin brothers.'

They smiled at each other, but didn't volunteer any information and I was too shy to ask.

One evening towards the end of my holiday, though, when it was mothy and dark as Gwladys walked me back to Gran's, I ventured to ask her about the handsome young men.

She seemed flustered. 'What young men?' 'The brothers in the photographs on the bedside tables.' 'Yes. Very nice young gentlemen,' she said then. 'Sons of a very good family. Not from round here at all.'

'What happened to them?'

'Killed in the war.'

'Both of them?'

'Both of them. Nice young men. Real gentlemen. Not from these parts, of course.'

'Poor Miss Hester and Miss Louise.'

'Yes indeed. 1944. Ten years ago now, very near. And never anyone else after.'

'Gran told me that my Uncle Bob was friendly with them once.'

She was furious. 'Nonsense. Your Uncle Bob was a labourer. He worked on the farm but he never came to the house. He knew his place, Bob did. Your Gran likes to boast, that's all. I'm turning back now. You can run from here, can't you.'

'Gwladys *was* in a stew when I told her about uncle Bob courting the sisters,' I told Gran.

'She knows nothing about it. She was in Swansea nursing her mother during the war. It was I who had to look after the sisters then.'

'Do you mean when their young men were killed?'

'Their young men? What young men are talking about now?'

'Real gentlemen, Gwladys said they were. Sons of a very good family.'

'Gwladys is getting soft in the head.'
Now that I had my interesting association with the Arwel sisters to sustain me, Gran didn't seem so much of a trial; indeed she often seemed nothing but a fairly harmless relic from an unhygienic past. Sometimes in the evening, I sat at her side on the old rexine sofa, leaning my head on her shoulder, almost able to ignore the dirty dishcloth smell coming from her.

'Tell me a secret, Gran.'

'What about?'

'You know. About the sisters. About their past. Tell me why they're different from other people.'

'I'll tell you when you're older.'

'Gran, you'll be dead when I'm older.'

She chuckled at that. She liked straight talk. She leaned forward, looked me straight in the eye and cleared her throat. 'They never had any men friends, real gentlemen or otherwise. They only had one man between them and he . . . he was an Italian prisoner of war.'

'Is that all?'

'Isn't that enough?'

'He was a handsome man, anyway. I saw his photo, two of his photos.'

'Married, of course.'

'So they were in disgrace, is that it?'

'You could say that, yes.'

I could see her hesitating about going on, but I squeezed her arm and gave her an imploring look.

'Their father found him in bed with them, you see. In between them, he said. That seemed to be the last straw. I don't think he'd have minded quite so much if he'd been either firmly on one side or the other, but there he was cuddled up between them. All three of them naked as babies, he said.'

'Naked?' I swallowed hard. Of course I knew about sexual intercourse, but I found certain of the details very unsavoury.

'Naked as new born babies.'

'And after the war, I suppose he went back to Italy?' I tried to keep the quiver out of my voice.

Gran paused again. 'No. No, sometime later he was found shot in Henblas woods.'

'Murdered? Do you mean murdered?'

'That's right. Murdered. The Italians weren't exactly loved at that time, especially the very handsome ones. No one found out who'd shot him. There were no clues. It could have been anybody, I suppose.'

'I think it was their father don't you, Gran, who murdered him.'

'It could have been their father. He had a massive heart attack six months later. It could have been guilt, I suppose.'

'Poor things. Poor Hester. Poor Louise.'

'Don't cry. You wanted the truth and now you must accept it.'

'And you had to look after them. Were they very unhappy?'

'They were, of course. Very unhappy.'

She glanced at me again, as though wondering how much more I could take. 'Go on,' I said.

'And pregnant as well. Very pregnant. Five or six months pregnant.'

'Both of them?'

'Both of them. Well, that's what happens when you lie naked in bed with a handsome young man, especially an Italian.'

'Both of them pregnant?'

'Yes.'

'Oh Gran, whatever happened to their little babies?'

'I looked after their babies, one boy, one girl, until they

were old enough to be adopted. And it was straight after that their father died.'

'Gran, it's a terrible story, a cruel story.'

'That's why I didn't want you to hear it.'

We were both silent for a while. I felt there was a hand twisting my stomach. I wanted to be sick, wanted to vomit up everything I'd heard.

'But they've still got each other, haven't they,' I said at last.

'Yes, they've still got each other, God help them, foolish as they are.'

I thought of them, their arms tightly clasped round each other's waists, repeating each other's sentences, spending hours laying out their dresses on the wide bed, deciding which to wear, trying on their lovely jewellery.

'Shall I spend the whole day with them tomorrow, Gran? Because it's my last day? They said I could.'

'Then I suppose you can. Silly girl. Go to bed now. You can come again next year . . . unless I'm dead before that, of course.'

I bent to kiss her good night. 'Silly girl,' she said again.

The Whirligig of Time

'And thus the whirligig of time brings in his revenges.'
Twelfth Night

I wouldn't have recognized him. Twenty-five years is a long time, and he looked so much younger. Now, I mean. In the Sixth, he had looked faded, tired, middle-aged. Now middle-aged, an eminent consultant, he looked a carefree playboy. His hair was still grey, but steel grey, distinguished, elegantly styled. He was expensively tanned. He looked as though he spent his lunchtimes at a gymnasium. At school, he'd worn small round spectacles and was excused games. He arrived so early every morning and remained behind so late, that no one ever met him on the way. I used to swear he came by some subterranean passage, never exposed to temptations like fresh air. Or girls.

He was brilliant, of course. He could work out all the most complicated calculations in his head. He knew every chemical formula, had by heart all the laws and tables that even our teachers had to look up.

I was the dumb blonde of the form, but he treated me very kindly; would, for instance, provide me with concise notes so that I could get my homework done while I was on prefect duty before lessons. 'Whatever were you doing last night?' he used to ask me, and I, thinking of sessions of fairly heavy petting in a certain park not so far away, used to say, 'Something very naughty.' 'Oh, washing your hair again, I suppose,' he would say, pushing his long, grey, greasy hair away from his glasses.

I teased him unmercifully. Even when he was taking the greatest trouble to explain something to me, I had to make capital of it. 'Please Sir, may I stay in with Neddy during break? He says he's got something very interesting to show me.' The class used to laugh, of course, and that meant much more to me than his embarrassment.

He remained devoted to me though, finding the apparatus I needed, setting up my experiments, adjusting the equipment. 'Not here, Neddy, how dare you!' I used to say, slapping his hands down from my microscope.

Unfortunately, he couldn't help me during my A-levels, which I failed while he won a major scholarship to Cambridge.

We didn't meet again till last week. Last week, at some charity committee, an attractive, glossy young woman whom I'd never seen before introduced herself to me. 'Antonia Langford,' she said, shooting out a small gloved hand in my direction. 'My husband was at school with you. Edward Langford.' I think I had the grace to blush. 'He watches everything you do on television. He's a terrific fan. He'd simply adore to meet you again.' The kindness of a pretty young wife to an old flame fifteen years her senior.

'I look very different on the telly,' I said. 'He'll be very disappointed.' I had little or no make-up on that afternoon, my hair was scraped back. She didn't contradict me.

'There was an old film of yours on Midnight Movie the other night. We had people to dinner, but at half past eleven he got our maid to come in and say there'd been a call from the hospital. Whereupon he crept upstairs to watch it in the bedroom.'

'That doesn't sound like . . . er . . . Edward. He used to be rather scornful of . . .'

She didn't let me finish. She didn't seem interested in what her husband used to be. 'Could you come to have

dinner with us sometime? Edward would be knocked out.'
Silly cow.

I gave her my telephone number, but I didn't expect to
hear from her. (Guess who I saw this afternoon? Your old
heart-throb, Rachel Harvey. My God, had she gone to seed.)

That same evening, though, he rang. Neddy.

'Come to dinner,' he said. 'How dare you hide yourself
away when you live so close.' He didn't sound at all like
the Neddy Langford I remembered. His voice was deep and
dark. 'Ultimatum,' he said. 'This coming Friday or else . . .'

I didn't want to go. I liked the idea of the old Neddy
worshipping from afar. The dynamic consultant surgeon,
Edward Langford, seemed too much of a challenge. I felt
my age.

I went, of course.

As soon as I saw him – I've already described him – and
his circle of friends: gracious-living, rich, middle-aged
consultants all on their second wives who were young,
bored and obviously getting their kicks elsewhere, I knew
what the outcome would be and started looking forward to
it. This time my lengthy and thorough preparations hadn't
been in vain. This time, my little black dress – by Galliano –
and the costliest perfume in the world weren't going to let
me down.

Throughout the evening as I ate and drank my way
through the Cordon Bleu menu and fine wines and talked
brightly, in the way television personalities (Best Comedy
Actress 1982) are supposed to talk, I was conscious of the
invitation in his eyes turning to pleading and entreaty. And
when I got a moment's opportunity, I fantasized about our
love-making, wondering which of the two Edwards I should
encounter later on – shy and devoted or sophisticated and
brash. I didn't much care, I seemed to like both. And my
God, they both seemed to like me.

Back in my own flat, my own bed, I was even more confused about him. Sometimes I seemed to sense, though not see, the boy I used to know behind the brave new image. His talk was light and urbane, but there seemed all the passion of first love, all the regrets of a lifetime in his love-making. On my part? On my part, I have to confess that I'd never before felt such an attraction and closeness to anyone. It was as though I'd loved him, body and soul, through all the years we'd been apart, as though I could love him for ever; the cynicism I'd cultivated for years had completely disappeared, I was in love. I shivered with the terror of it.

'How long can you stay?'

'As long as you'll have me.'

'What about your wife?'

'She's very understanding.'

'How terrible. I was never an understanding wife. The younger generation is so hard.'

'How many times were you married?'

'Once.'

'Why didn't it work?'

'It did work. It didn't work for ever, but it worked fairly well for quite a long time.'

'How long?'

'Nine years. Or was it nineteen? A long time.'

'Why haven't you married again?'

'I want too much' (Brain as well as brawn. Love as well as lust. Someone like you, Neddy.) 'Do you always ask all these questions?' (Someone like you.)

'It's my scientific training, I suppose.'

'Do you want a notebook?'

'No.'

'Do you want anything? Anything else?'

He sat up and looked at me again. A different look. Tender. Heart-breaking. 'Oh Rachel, how I loved you. You'll

never know how much I loved you. Oh God, Rachel,
I loved you.'

All safely and firmly in the past tense, cleanly and
honestly in the past tense.

'If I could turn the clock back, things would be different,'
I said. 'I often thought about you. You were the one I
remembered out of everyone. Honestly.' I licked my index
finger and crossed his heart. His body was strong and
hard. I couldn't say more without breaking down.

We kissed again. (Did he think I kissed everyone as I
kissed him? Long, long tongue kisses.)

'I think you ought to go now, Neddy. It's four o'clock.' (I
felt he wanted to leave.)

'You won't get rid of me without a struggle, you know.'

'Don't start being kind.' (It's bad enough without your
pity.)

'Rachel.'

'When you've gone I'll cry myself to sleep. Will that cancel
all the times I made fun of you?'

'I suppose so. I suppose that will make it fair. We'll call
that fair.' He stroked my face, gazed into my eyes. With
great affection, it seemed to me. 'I'd better go,' he said. 'I
suppose I'd better go.'

But we clung together for another long moment. I couldn't
decide whether he was crying too, or whether they were
my tears on his cheeks.

Home Sweet Home

My Dad is a soldier in Africa and he lives in a tent. My brothers Alfie and Dougie draw pictures of yellow sands and palm trees and big tanks and aeroplanes smoking in the sky. I don't like to do war pictures, but sometimes I can see them inside my head and I don't like that.

My Dad doesn't have a gun of his own over his shoulder, but there's a big gun in the front of the tank with a little window over the top so he's more safe and the bangs aren't so loud. They try to shoot the soldier on the other side of a long line they draw in the sands and it's the war.

Alfie and Dougie show me Africa on the map, a pink place in the middle of a lot of blue sea.

We went to the sea once on a holiday and we stayed in a little wooden house with sea-shells over the door and we had ice-cream and tea in a café, but where my Dad is, it's much, much further away. It's Africa. The bad soldiers are Eyties and the good soldiers are English like my Dad and Miss Hunniford says I should be proud of him. When you're proud of someone, it's feeling warm inside when you think about them. I think about my Dad but sometimes I can't remember him.

When my Mum sends a letter to my Dad, me and Alfie and Dougie send him some pictures and best love, but we have to share a small piece of paper because you can only send two and my Mum has one all to herself. She does joined-up writing with a row of Xs at the bottom. Xs mean kisses. Kisses aren't silly. Sometimes I do Xs for my Dad. Alfie and Dougie draw lots of tanks and aeroplanes smoking in the sky, but I draw an armchair with a frill all round the bottom and a big fire in the grate and over it I put Home Sweet Home because Miss Hunniford says that's a very nice message for a soldier in the war and I copy it out on my slate three times so I know all the letters. A big 'h' is like the bottom of a ladder and a little 'w' goes down, up, down, up. Alfie and Dougie are nine years old and eight years old and I am five and three quarters and my birthday is quite soon after Christmas. After my birthday I will be six.

Sometimes we have bombs in the night and they are very noisy and the smell goes up your nose, but Miss Hunniford says it's silly to be afraid because the air-raid wardens are there to look after you. When there's bombs in the night a lot of children don't go to school but me and Alfie and Dougie go because we have hot milk at playtime and singing in the hall instead of writing and sums.

My mother has a job looking after Mrs Cooper next door because she's bad with her nerves and has to rest in a chair with her legs up and sometimes she cries. Miss Hunniford says that when grown-ups cry it's because of the war and the bombs, but my Mum says it's her time of life. Children should always be brave if they can. Alfie and Dougie are nearly always brave. When it's an air-raid they play fighters and bombers but I don't like the noise.

Mrs Cooper's tears pour down her cheeks but she doesn't sniff. She has a nice face but when she cries it gets pink and creased. Her legs have mauve patches on and Mum says not to keep looking, but you do because they're up on a footstool and you can't help it. She gives my Mum half-a-crown every day and sometimes some slices of meat. Her smell is a bit dusty like the inside of the plasticine cupboard at school, but my Mum says she's a real lady. Sometimes she lets me cut out pictures from her magazine and sometimes I can turn the little white mangle in her kitchen.

Mr Cooper works down Small Heath in a factory making munitions which is guns and bombs and my Mum makes him his tea. My Mum calls Mr Cooper, Eric. He has got a lot of shiny white hair and a nice smile which I don't like. Alfie and Dougie get cigarette cards off him and he sometimes lets them borrow his knife. Alfie and Dougie like Mr Cooper because he tells them how to make bombs, but I don't believe it.

Our raids are getting worse and last week Evelyn King lost her mother. It means she was killed by a bomb not lost like your crayons or your chalk. We had to do hands together, close your eyes for her. A noise came in my throat and it sounded like somebody laughing and Miss Hunniford looked over at me but sometimes you can't help making a noise in your throat like laughing and it's not laughing at all. Evelyn King is in Alfie's class. She used to have two long pigtails but now it's tied back in a piece of black braid because her Gran can't do everything. She has got a nice name, Evelyn King. All her class have to be kind to her. Alfie gave her quite a lot of aniseed balls . . . Anyway, I don't like aniseed balls.

Sometimes you can't get cherry lips and rainbow chews because it's the war. There's lots of food, like dinners, you can't get because it's the war, but I like hot toast and dripping and best of all chips from the chip shop on the corner with salt and vinegar on. In the playground the big girls sing, 'A penn'oth o' chips to grease yer lips and out goes you.' The big girls skip very fast and the rope thwacks the ground like a big whip and I would never like to dodge in and out the ropes like the big girls in case they'd hit the backs of my legs.

You can't buy a penn'oth of chips now because it's tuppence. That's because it's the war, but they give you salt and vinegar. The salt is crackly and it bounces off the chips.

I like the little crispy ones at the top and Alfie likes the big soft ones so sometimes we swap, but the big ones are bigger. Sometimes we have soup out of a tin but you can only have potato soup because it's the war. Alfie can remember when you could have chocolate biscuits with silver paper on.

I have to wear Dougie's vests and his shirts, but my Granny knits me a new jumper and a pixie hood to match and I have a plaid skirt. Plaid is lots of colours crossing over and under. My Granny lives in the country and she can't come to see us because she's afraid of the sirens going off. I could go and live with her if I wanted, but I'd miss my Mum and Miss Hunniford. They have a school in the country but no chip shop. I don't think I'd like to live in the country because I don't like cows or farmers. I think I would miss Alfie and Dougie too.

I don't mind the bombs too much. We have to sleep in the cupboard under the stairs when it's an air-raid. My Mum calls it the glory-hole but it's really a big cupboard. We have put a mattress there instead of the brooms and boxes of firewood and we have to sleep very close together and Mum says we're like sardines in a tin. You can still smell the firewood. Sometimes we have sardines for our Sunday tea and I like crunching their little silver bones. Sometimes my Mum only stays long enough to give me a cuddle because she's too squashed, but I don't like it when she goes because I get cold next to the door.

Sometimes Mr Cooper calls in to see if we're all fit. He says, 'Are you all fit?' and my Mum says 'How is Mrs Cooper tonight?' And she's usually very bad with her nerves and Mr Cooper has to give her one of her pills so that she can go to sleep, or sometimes two.

Next door they have a dining-room as well as a front room and Mr Cooper has boarded up the window of the dining-room so that it's quite safe, though not as safe as the cupboard under the stairs but Mrs Cooper won't hear of sleeping there. If you won't hear of doing something it means you don't want to do it and you won't. Mrs Cooper sleeps in the dining-room. A dining-room is really for having your tea in, but it's a lot of extra work, my Mum says.

Sometimes I've already fallen asleep when Mr Cooper comes to ask, 'Are you all fit?' but I wake up when the door creaks open and my Mum shines the torch and I can see his shiny white hair and then my Mum creeps out to make him a cup of tea and I wish he'd stay in his own house but I don't say it. Sometimes he has to go out all night to be an air-raid warden, but most of the time he doesn't because of Mrs Cooper with her bad nerves and I wish he had to go out every night.

One day I told Miss Hunniford about Mr Cooper coming in every time there's an air-raid on and she said he was a very kind neighbour, but I thought about Mrs Cooper left on her own. Your time of life can be as bad as an illness my Mum says. And sometimes Mr Cooper stays a long, long time with my Mum because I can hear them talking and sometimes laughing in the kitchen.

Miss Hunniford has got a new ring and the other teachers crowd round her to have a look at it. It's an engagement ring. A man gives it to you and it means you're going to get married. When you get married you have a little house and a baby in a pram. I hope somebody gives me an engagement ring.

Dorothy Trig from Class Five asked Miss Hunniford when she was getting married and she said after the war. Lots and lots of things are going to happen after the war, our front window will be mended, we'll have a new wireless set that works and perhaps a little white mangle like Mrs Cooper's and my Dad will come home from Africa. I hope it will be soon.

Sometimes Alfie brings me home past the bomb sites. He's not allowed to play out until he's brought me safe home, but he shouts to his friends as we go past and they tell him to hurry up. They slide down the bannisters when there are any stairs left and they play in the cellars and sometimes they find things. One day Alfie found a tea-caddy with tea in and he gave it to my Mum and his friend Len found a pair of tongs. I don't know what tongs are but I like saying the word. Tongs.

There are cats on the bomb sites. When they see you they run away as though you're going to throw a stone at them though you're not. Alfie says they can look after themselves but I don't think it's fair to leave your cat behind, even if you have been bombed. I wish we could take one home but Alfie says no one could catch one. They've gone wild, he says, and frightened of everyone.

Sometimes I get frightened. One night last week I woke up freezing cold in the glory-hole because Alfie and Dougie had got all the blankets and I couldn't get them back. And then I could hear a bomb making a whooshing noise and there was a bang like a big house being dropped down on the street outside, so near that our house shook and I was waiting for it to fall down. I counted to ten and then another ten and it didn't fall down and then I felt a bit braver but not very brave and I was still shivering all over and the boys were still fast asleep so I crept out to find my Mum though I'm not allowed to when there's an air-raid on. And she wasn't in the kitchen having a cup of tea, so I tiptoed up the stairs though I'm not allowed to do that either.

The lino was icy cold and it was pitch dark on the landing, but I felt my way to Mum's bedroom and I had my hand on the doorknob when I heard a little noise, as quiet as mice scratching and all of a sudden I knew for sure that Mr Cooper was in there with her. And I didn't like it, I didn't like it a bit. I wanted to cry and shout at him to go back to his house, but my voice wouldn't come so I didn't do anything, only crept downstairs.

I could hear lots of people in the street rushing about as though it was daytime. Everything was the wrong way round. Miss Hunniford says we must trust in God, but I don't like Evelyn King's mother getting killed or those thin cats on the bomb sites or Mrs Cooper crying with her nerves or things the wrong way round.

When I got back I woke Alfie and Dougie up by hitting them and then we had a fight for the blankets. Dougie's elbow caught me in the eye and I cried and then he started to cry as well because Alfie landed him one, and then my Mum came down to see what was wrong and I said, 'I hate Mr Cooper.' And she said, 'He just popped in to see if we were all fit, pet, and when it's the All Clear he'll go back to his own house and I'll make us some cocoa.'

And then it was the All Clear and we had a mug of cocoa each and my Mum crept in with us and we got nice and warm and then we all went back to sleep.

And the next day we were all very tired but we went to school again because it's the war and that is what you have to do.

Maid in Heaven

You felt sorry for the old maids. There were several in the village when you were a girl. They'd missed what was then considered the best thing in life and had to manage as well as they could without it; living at home, looking after elderly parents, working on a smallholding or in one of the shops in town, knitting endless jumpers for nephews and nieces in their spare time and going meekly to chapel on a Sunday.

You liked them on the whole. They weren't as bossy as the mothers, and the ones who worked in shops sometimes gave you a sweet if you hung about long enough.

One or two of the old maids tended to be figures of fun. Ada Morris, for instance, because she never gave up, still going to town on a Saturday night, curled and high-heeled and lipsticked, whistling after soldiers, they said, and screaming with laughter if any of them as much as turned to look at her.

Evadne Browne (Browne with an E, she always said, when you wrote down her name) was another eccentric; English for a start and nearly six foot tall. She'd come to the village for a weekend and stayed twenty-two years. There was a whisper that she'd been jilted at the altar. You used to imagine her waiting in the church like a sad, white flagpole. Miss Browne with an E didn't talk to anyone, but you always went to her first when you were collecting for the Missionary, because she gave you half a crown and you could only get pennies out of everybody else, and if you got fifteen shillings they gave you a book, too boring to read, but coveted for all that.

But Jennie Williams was neither pitied nor scorned. Her family had once been important, she'd been left a bit of money and she was one of the liveliest members of the village. About her, you felt that she simply hadn't wanted to get married – and who'd be a match for her anyway? Jenny Williams went some way towards making spinster-hood respectable.

When we had concerts to get Comforts for the Forces, she was bold enough to trade on her status, treating the village to one of her Old Maid monologues.

As soon as she appeared on stage in an old-fashioned black costume which had belonged to her mother, thick black stockings and lace-up boots, the applause was hearty – and that before she'd said a word.

'I'm Jenny Williams,' she'd begin in a flat, expressionless voice. 'I'm an old maid.' More applause. 'Oh, I get along all right, only I don't have anyone to light my fire. The minister calls every week, mind . . . to have a cup of tea. And as far as other things are concerned, what you've never had, you never miss . . . So they say.'

You didn't understand half her jokes, but you clapped and stamped your feet and whistled just like everybody else. She had more encores by far than our contralto, Lisa Emlyn, though she'd once sung in the National.

At Christmas there was a special concert when all the chapel children, even those from down Mill Bank who'd only started coming to Sunday School at the beginning of December, had a present from the Christmas tree.

In spite of the war, we had good presents, but our Father Christmas was always a hopeless failure, a mumbling old man with a slipping beard, that no one, not even the babies in Class 1, believed in.

Jenny Williams changed all that. One year, she came on in a little red cloak and bonnet. 'I'm Mother Christmas,' she said. 'My old man's been called up. Yes. he's gone from under my feet. Good job, too. He was always an old nuisance. And mean. Ooo. He used to spend more on those dirty old reindeers than he did on me. Did you think he'd bought you those presents last year? No, it was the Ladies Sewing Circle. All he ever did was show off in his red suit. And that beard. It wasn't real. No. Did you think it was real? Of course you didn't.'

Mother Christmas was a huge success.

Jenny Williams had a low, chuckling laugh, lovely to hear, which was just as well because she laughed a great deal. She laughed when she came last in the Village Show, which she always did. She used to send in the flattest, sorriest Victoria sponges you ever saw and bramble jelly that wasn't even set. And there she'd be, laughing away at the curt notes the adjudicator left at the side of her exhibits. 'Well, somebody's got to be last,' she used to say.

She had a little black-and-white dog with a round face and a tail that stuck up like a flag. Bobby, she called him, Bobby Williams, and he was jaunty and full of fun, just like her. She took him everywhere. 'Any room for me and Bobby?' she used to call out to the bus conductor – and he always let them on, though he might have refused other people at the previous stop.

Anyway, one terrible day, Bobby was run over by a coal lorry reversing down Brynglas Lane, and it nearly broke her heart, but luckily some evacuees came from Liverpool the very next week, and she had one of those to take his place.

Rosie Tucker, her evacuee was called.

You and your friend, Mair, tried hard to be nice to Rosie, you really did, but it was awfully difficult, she was the sort of girl who just couldn't help being a nuisance.

She had wispy, hay-coloured hair, round blue eyes that

never seemed to blink and long flailing arms and legs. She trailed around after you with an everlasting, 'Wait for me, wait for me, oh please wait for me.' She fell into brooks, she fell off trees, she told tales.

She always had colds; even in summer, the runny nose and the long purposeful sniff. She was always losing things, and you and Mair had to go looking for them because she 'was only a little 'vacuee who didn't know her way around.'

She was a proper trial to you and Mair, one way and another. But Jenny Williams idolized her and wouldn't have a word spoken against her. She was always on her side.

She treated her like a little princess. She spent all her coupons buying her the most gorgeous clothes; pleated skirts and black patent-leather shoes and coats with velvet collars. She was always having new hair ribbons and pixie hoods, however many she lost. That girl even had a dressing-gown.

She even had a birthday party.

In your village, you had Sunday School parties at Christmas with jellies and Swiss rolls, and an outing to the sea in the summer, but to have a party all to yourself was unheard of.

Anyway, that's what she had. And Mair and you and six or seven other girls from Standard Three had to go to it, and had to take her a present each as well, a hankie or a bottle of scent.

And did she appreciate her good fortune? Not her. She did nothing but show off from start to finish. 'I want to cut the cake.' 'I want to play I-spy.' 'I want Eira Jones to sit next to me.' 'I want, I want.' It was really embarrassing.

And Jenny Williams giving in to her about everything and laughing at all her silly antics and hugging her whenever she wasn't winning every single game.

It was difficult not to hate Rosie, but you couldn't quite do that. She was too soft, perhaps. 'Gwirion' was my mother's word for her, which is half-way between innocent and simple, but coming down on the simple side.

But simple or not, that girl certainly managed to get everything she could possibly want.

Except for one thing. There were lots of weddings in the village at that time; soldiers being sent abroad and wanting someone to send them letters, I suppose. And Rosie wanted to be a flower-girl at a wedding.

Mair and you had been flower-girls three times each in just over eighteen months – once you had a long frock, you were quite in demand in those days – and she always wanted to do everything like you and Mair.

Well, a second cousin of Jenny Williams's was getting married, and she thought she could persuade her into having Rosie as one of her attendants, but this cousin refused point blank. She already had two lined up, she said, nieces of the bridegroom, pretty little girls with dark curly hair, and she wasn't having a third who didn't match in any way, and that was that.

Then Jenny Williams wrote to a friend in Carmarthen who had a daughter getting married, but though she tried to bribe her with a dozen eggs and half a pound of farm butter, she had no better luck there; the cake was already made and iced, thank you very much. Quite curt.

To be honest, Rosie wasn't your idea of a flower-girl. It wasn't that she was ugly, not exactly, but you could as soon picture a moony calf following the bride up the aisle.

However, she was dreadfully disappointed, and to make matters worse, Jenny Williams had some beautiful shiny pink material she'd promised to have made up for her.

You had to feel sorry for her in the end. Not that being a flower-girl was all that marvellous; it was only a lot of standing still, having to smile, having to do this, not being allowed to do that; but it was no use trying to tell her that. It was the one thing in the world she wanted, and the one thing Jenny Williams couldn't give her.

I think it was early in February 1944, and in a savagely cold spell of snow and ice, that Rosie was taken bad with appendicitis. Dr Parry phoned for an ambulance straight away, but it was held up by six-foot snow drifts and when they'd managed to get her to the hospital, her appendix had burst and she was almost done for.

Jenny Williams was half-mad with worry. Whenever you saw her, she was dabbing her eyes or wringing her hands. Not a smile out of her now, never mind a chuckle.

It was touch and go. That's what people said. Touch and go. It meant she could die.

You imagined her lying white and still in her coffin. You practised making wreaths with moss and the first primroses. You prayed; haunted by all the times you'd been spiteful to her. Touch and go. Oh please, dear Jesus Christ, let her get better.

Then at long last, your prayers were answered; she started to recover.

And when she came home – after two months in hospital instead of two weeks like everybody else – you and Mair were the first invited to go to see her.

And there she was, sitting by the fire in the front room, with a rug over her knees, looking like somebody's grandmother. You had a lump like a potato in your throat. You said you were glad to see her. You were.

And the first thing she said – listen to this – was that she was going to be a bridesmaid; a chief bridesmaid, if you please, no modest flower-girl role for her. It was still a bit of a secret, the wedding, but it was going to be in June or July, when she was really well again, and you'd be allowed to come to see her walking up the aisle in her lovely long pink frock and satin slippers.

You thought she was making it up, something she'd dreamed up under the anaesthetic, and so did your mother, only she said for goodness' sake not to contradict her, in her state of health.

Anyway, it turned out to be true.

It seems far-fetched to say that Jenny Williams got married just so that Rosie Tucker, her evacuee, could be a bridesmaid, but that's what everyone in our village thought.

Good gracious, they said, this fellow she was marrying, this Ifor Lewis, he'd been courting her ten years before and been turned down flat. An unsuccessful painter and decorator he was ten years ago, and that's what he was still, pushing a hand-cart around town with his ladders and his pots of paint, only just making ends meet, no house, no motor-car, no expectations. What had he got to offer her they asked one another.

But he wasn't a bad-looking chap, for all that. And if his hair had disappeared from the middle of his head, it grew outwards like two white wings at the sides. He had a nice friendly smile, too, and if he was being made use of, he certainly looked as though he was enjoying it, every minute of it.

Not that he had much of a part on the wedding day. Nor did the bride, come to that. Jenny Williams wore a plain navy-blue two-piece and a little cream straw hat that would do for chapel after.

It was Rosie's day. She'd had her hair permed, if you please, so that it looked like a bird's nest, and she had a wreath of tiny rosebuds perched on the top of it. She had new net gloves and white kid shoes and her pink dress was frilled and flounced and so wide that she could hardly get through the chapel door. She looked remarkable – that was the word people used – remarkable, and very, very happy.

And that's the end of the story.

Well, people get married for all sorts of reasons; because they have to, for money, for property, for convenience, love, companionship, passion. If Jenny Williams got married to give her little evacuee something to live for, that seems as good a reason as most. The marriage turned out as happy as most, too.

You can still remember that wedding. 'Well, it'll be all right won't it? After all, we're both getting on, so it's not a life sentence. And he's not too bad, is he? In a decent suit, he's quite passable. And he loves children. Oh, don't be silly! I only meant Rosie. We're not expecting a miracle. Please God.' Her lovely laugh.

Fifty years on, you still remember that laugh.

Too Much Excitement

It was Mrs Courtnay's eighty-fifth birthday. She'd had her hair set and rinsed the previous day, she'd had a good night's sleep, so that she felt moderately well and not unattractive.

She was anxious to look her best. Birthdays were becoming important again, as they'd been when she was a child, and she was going to her son's for lunch. Betty, one of the cleaning ladies, had pressed her best dress and jacket and laid them out ready for her. Some of the residents complained that the cleaners were abrupt and unhelpful, but Mrs Courtnay always found them obliging. They recognized something in her, she told herself.

She looked about her at the large, high-ceilinged room, once the master bedroom of the Cedars. It was fortunate that Major Dingley, who had occupied it when she'd first arrived, had agreed to move to a smaller, and of course cheaper room at the back of the house; no other would have suited her so well. It was quiet, it overlooked the garden, it had a certain grandeur that the other rooms lacked. Furthermore, Mrs Weston treated her with special consideration, allowing her to have her meals there when she didn't feel up to the dining-room. The flat in Knightsbridge had become too much for her after the death of her companion; the succession of Spanish maids the agency sent had been quite unsuitable for someone used to – well – a certain *deference*.

She glanced at her silk dress. 'The new length,' Edna Gregory had exclaimed when she had seen it on earlier (if only she'd known how old it was). 'What a stylish dress, the new length and the new colour. They call that shade banana, don't they.'

'I believe so,' Mrs Courtnay had answered. (Banana!)

Poor Edna prided herself on her knowledge of the latest fashion; was always reading snippets from the *Telegraph* and the *Lady* to anyone who'd listen.

'You should wear it with black, a black georgette scarf. That's the latest look, I believe.'

'Black is ageing,' Mrs Courtnay had answered firmly. 'I shall wear it quite plain. With a gold clip, perhaps, at the neck.'

'And your lovely straw hat, dear, and your lizard shoes. Shall I put a duster over your shoes for you?'

'No thank you, I can manage nicely.' With a little nod, Edna was dismissed.

Mrs Courtnay kept her lizard shoes in several layers of blue tissue paper which kept out the light and the dust. Her late companion, Miss Wilks, had once ventured the opinion that a plastic bag might be adequate. But Mrs Courtnay didn't subscribe to the doctrine of the adequate.

She felt a spasm of physical pleasure as she touched the shoes, so supple and elegant. She had long, slim feet, a source of great pride, and she'd had the shoes made for her, oh, many years ago; certainly before the war. And they would outlast her without a doubt. She put that thought out of her mind and buffed them with a velvet pad. It was ten o'clock.

At half past ten she started to dress.

She decided not to go downstairs for coffee, nor to listen to Morning Service on her wireless; she would concentrate on looking her best. She brushed and combed the tight silver-blue curls and waves, then patted a thick layer of powder on her wrinkled, slightly furry skin. She tidied her rather shaggy eyebrows. They drooped a little now, but were still dark, and had once been considered her best feature. (Black wings, Arthur had called them.)

Putting on her lipstick was the most difficult part, her hand being rather less than steady, and the outline of her lips not quite firm. It took her a little time, but the job was well done, no smudging except for a little on her teeth which was easy to wipe off.

She sat for a moment or two, her hands folded in her lap, regarding herself in the mirror.

There was a tap at the door.

'Come in.'

It was, as she expected, Edna Gregory. A little cry: 'Oh you look so smart!'

Mrs Courtnay couldn't help a slight smile, though she had meant to be severe; Edna could be forward at times.

'You look so young. When is your son coming?'

'At twelve. Just as usual.'

'Isn't there anything I can do for you? I'm quite free now until lunch-time. Can I fetch you some of my French perfume? The one I had from my cousin Mabel last Christmas?'

'No thank you. I have some of my usual cologne on my handkerchief.'

'Shall I reach your hat?'

'It's on the chair.'

'You've done everything,' Edna Gregory pouted. She was one of the youngest in the Rest Home, only seventy-three, and loved to be busy. Her face, round and unlined, was like the face of a very old child.

Mrs Courtnay relented. 'You could pass me my jewel box from the dressing table, if you would.' Edna, she couldn't help thinking, would have made an excellent lady's maid.

'Thank you. Now, shall I wear my gold clip or my

pearls?' (The heavy clip had been her mother's. Arthur had brought her the perfectly matched single row of pearls from the East.)

'Oh, but can't you wear both,' Edna said. 'After all it is your birthday.'

'The pearls, I think,' Mrs Courtnay said, ignoring her.

The drive, through quiet residential roads, woodlands and parks, was pleasant as always.

Piers talked on the usual subjects; his garden and the incompetence of the old-age pensioner who helped him with it, the difficulties he was currently encountering with his work at the Foreign Office; the warning he'd had to give the new junior minister. But even as he lapsed into his customary absent-minded silence, his mother recognized in him all the small signs of inward pleasure; the quick self-satisfied look in the mirror, the slight adjustment to his tie, the way he threw back his shoulders and straightened his back; things were going well for him. Well, he deserved it. He worked hard. Always had. What a pity, she thought, as she so often did, that he's made such an unsuitable marriage.

Mrs Courtnay felt that she would have been ready to forgive Laura her humble background if she made any attempts to bridge the gap between them. But Laura made none. She refused to cultivate the right people; what entertaining she did was worse than useless; buffet suppers for twenty to thirty people, where any of Piers's distinguished colleagues had to rub shoulders with her arty, pseudo-intellectual friends. People they should have known, the sons and daughters of the people she and Arthur had known, had dropped them. 'They were dull, Mother,' Laura would say, as though that had any significance. One Sunday, she, the daughter of a District Commissioner, the widow of a high-ranking diplomat, had eaten lunch, at her own son's house, with a man who wore no socks.

Her grandchildren, two boys and a girl, were well enough in appearance, but had no idea of correct behaviour, being rowdy and completely unrepressed. She could sense that Piers was very often embarrassed by their behaviour.

And now Laura was set on encouraging the eldest, Jonathan, to go to an Art School. When Mrs Courtnay had mentioned family traditions Laura had said, quite gaily, that they might start another. Miranda wanted to go to a medical school where she'd learn many unpleasant things that no lady should be called upon to know. Richard was only fourteen but his only interest in life was playing the drums.

'Are the children well?' she asked her son.

'Very well,' he said. Probably only she would have noticed the tinge of bitterness in his voice.

Lunch, on that birthday Sunday, was much better organized than usual, being both formal and festive. The table was properly laid for once, with decent cutlery and glasses. There were even flowers, though pushed just anyhow into vases; there was champagne, no less, for the birthday toast.

After they had drunk her health, Laura raised her glass again. That day, she said, they had a double cause for celebration. Listen everyone. Piers was to receive a knighthood in the next day's honours list.

'My darling boy,' Mrs Courtnay said, raising her glass. Tears of pride dazzled her eyes. She had been right about the undercurrent of excitement she'd recognized in him. She thought about him at the Palace. How proud his father would have been. 'My darling boy,' she said again. She accepted another glass of champagne.

Even the children, she was pleased to note, seemed impressed by the news, seemed quiet and anxious to please. For the first time she wondered if Richard had inherited just a little of his father's quiet charm. He was usually the first to rush away from the table. On this occasion he was being quite civilized, even smiling from time to time.

'May I bring Zac along for some of Grannie's birthday cake?' Miranda was asking. (When, before, had she asked permission to bring home her rowdy friends? What sort of people would call a child Zac?)

Jonathan, sitting on his grandmother's right, actually initiated a conversation about a film he'd been to see. 'Of course, you lived in India, didn't you?' She was encouraged to tell him a little about the Delhi she remembered, the princes she'd met, and he'd seemed interested.

After coffee, Piers took her to sit in the garden and after a few minutes Laura came out to join them. 'It was a lovely lunch, dear,' she told her, deciding to be gracious. After all, she'd learnt to get along with Edna Gregory. A certain lowering of standards was inevitable in these difficult days.

When they returned to the house, Mrs Courtnay had a little sleep in an armchair by the french windows.

When she woke, it was four o'clock. She had a touch of indigestion – the lamb, perhaps, wasn't as well-cooked as it might have been – but the splendid news about Piers kept her in good spirits. Not even Miranda's friend with the outlandish name, who shouted at her as though she was both deaf and senile, was allowed to upset her that day.

The birthday cake was shop-made and tasted of sawdust, but was, in all fairness, prettily decorated, if you cared for such things. She crumbled a little on her plate and sipped her tea. Miranda's foolish friend picked out 'Happy Birthday to You' on the piano and she managed to smile at him.

After she had finished her second cup of tea she turned to look at the clock. Sometimes when the weather was fine, Piers took her to Evensong before driving her back to the Cedars. It was their time alone together – Laura didn't attend church and naturally didn't try to influence the children to do so – and the highlight of the week.

'I'm afraid I can't take you to church this evening, Mother,' Piers said, noticing her glance at the clock. 'We're going out for a bit of a celebration later on. Will you mind if I run you back a little earlier than usual?'

'Of course not, dear.'

She minded, of course she did, but was prepared to be tolerant that day. 'I'm quite ready,' she said as soon as the tea was cleared away. 'After all, I shall want time to tell Mrs Weston and Miss Gregory the good news.'

They all accompanied her to the car, even the feeble-minded Zac, and she managed her goodbyes, stiff but perfectly courteous. She inclined her cheek for Laura's kiss.

Piers, solicitous as always, helped her into the car. After closing her door, he turned to his wife. 'Goodbye, Lady Courtnay,' she heard him say.

Lady Courtnay. The words exploded in her head.

She stared at Laura. An insignificant little woman, dressed in garish, off-the-peg clothes suitable only for a shop gel.

She looked disdainfully at her grandchildren; with that mother they would never be anything but ordinary and undistinguished, the dreadful Zac a fitting companion for them.

Throughout the drive home she sat upright and silent.

Several times Piers tried to start a conversation, but each time she cut him off quite abruptly. 'Too much excitement,' he told himself.

When Mrs Courtnay got back to her room, she eased off her precious lizard shoes and kicked them under the bed. She would never wear them again.

A House of One's Own

I'm Liverpool really, proper Scouse, but I've lived here in Brynhir – Brynhir, Gwynedd, North Wales – for nearly three months.

I own this house, this garden and that little stunted tree by the back wall.

Plenty of people own houses, I know, but for me it's a near-miracle because I've never owned anything before, a bag or two of clothes, a box of kitchen stuff, that's about it really.

When I got the letter from the solicitor I was struck dumb for a whole morning. I wanted to shout out the news to Anna Marie and Gina and Scottish Joe, the guys that shared the lousy flat I was living in, but I had no voice, not even a Scouse croak.

I was the sole legatee, the letter said, of Mr Trefor Roberts, 12 Clydwen Row, Brynhir, Gwynedd, and I could, at my convenience, pick up the key to the said property from Jenkins and Hedges, Solicitors, Hill Road, Caernarfon, Gwynedd.

Mr Trefor Roberts was my uncle Trefor, my great-uncle Trefor.

I could just about remember him. He visited us once when I was small. I think he only stayed a couple of days, probably because our house was a proper shambles, full of lodgers and wet washing, but for years after he used to send my Mum a ten shilling note every week, fastened to his letter by a neat little gold safety pin, and that didn't half make a difference to our life.

My father, my real father, also called Trefor Roberts, was his nephew. He married my mother straight after coming out of the army in 1946, his boat docked in Liverpool and he never went back to Wales after. I was born in 1951, the only child. He died of pneumonia when I was about two, and a bit after my mother married my step-dad who was the only father I can remember.

My great-uncle worked in one of these local quarries, I don't know which one, and when he came to visit us – well over thirty years ago – he already seemed old. Perhaps it was the heavy black suit he wore and the shiny black boots. He took me to the Sally Army Hall in Toxteth Road and I remember how loud he sang too. I think that was the only time he took me out, but he must have liked me a bit to leave me his house. Or I was his only living relative most like.

I've been thinking about him a hell of a lot since being in Brynhir, though of course I never gave him a thought before. Here, sleeping in his bed with the lumpy green and fawn mattress, sitting in his sagging old armchair, eating at his little scrubbed table, he seems almost alive and I wish I knew a bit more about him. He's got a little shelf of books, but I can't fuckin' read them because they're all in Welsh – people speak Welsh around here. But he wrote his diaries in English, so I've been looking through those. I was quite excited to discover them, forty black diaries, Letts diaries, the sort with a little pencil in a groove at the side, all laid out in perfect order in the top drawer of his bedroom chest. Unfortunately they're totally boring, all about his work at the quarry, the times of the blasting and so on, and on Sundays, the name of the preacher at the chapel he used to go to, the text of the sermon and the grade he gave it, usually a B. I found myself longing for a really bad sermon, something to liven up his week, but there was never a D. I suppose he was always too ready to think the best of everyone.

The other day I walked past the chapel he used to go to. Several of the chapels around here have been closed down and used as warehouses or arts and crafts places, but his, Bethel, is still a chapel, and though I've never had a religious thought in my head, I was quite pleased.

Why should I be spending my time reading this man's boring diaries and thinking about him? I'm totally fascinated by him, that's why. If he was a cannibal chief he couldn't be more different from anyone I know; so quiet, so methodical, so tidy, so decent.

My next door neighbour, a cross old woman called Netta Morris, scrubs her step every day and when it's not raining I go out to see if she'll deign to speak to me. Usually she'll only mutter a grudging g'morning, but once or twice she's managed to part with a scrap of information. 'Mr Roberts was a good neighbour,' she said on one occasion. 'He always carried my ash-can out the back.'

'Why did he never get married?'

'He had no need. Could do everything for himself. Cooking, washing, ironing, even mending.'

'Didn't he need a bit of company? A bit of comfort?'

She went back into her house at that question, closing the door firmly behind her.

I've always needed lots of company, lots of comfort. My mother was the same, but I'm worse. I've always needed lots of men and lots of booze, but for three months I've had neither. Being a property owner in Brynhir has filled my brain so that I don't need anything else, but it won't last. One of these days I'll pick up my giro, go down the pub on the pull and fill the house with men and loud sexy music and to hell with Netta Morris.

Last week I bought a large, dark green waterproof coat

which cost twenty-three pounds. I could hardly believe what I was doing. I've never before owned such a remarkably boring and hideous garment. Oh yes, I know it will be useful – it doesn't stop raining in this place – and practical too because it will hide all the tat underneath, but since when have I gone in for being dry and respectable? Perhaps it's due to losing so much weight; I'm almost human-shaped now, what with giving up the booze and the Chinese takeaways. I also bought a window cleaner called Mr Brite and some new bags for Uncle Trefor's old Hoover. Am I becoming a fuckin' housewife?

I've got to the 1959 diary and discovered that in March that year Uncle Trefor was faced with a problem. The owner of his house, a Richard Paul Mathias, died, leaving it to two of his cousins who are in dispute over the will so that he doesn't know who to send the rent to. In April he went to Caernarfon to take advice from a Mr Stanley Jenkins, solicitor, who tells him not to send it to anyone until the matter has been settled.

I'm in a cold sweat. Do the cousins of Richard Paul Mathias still own this house? Will I discover that this damp three-roomed terraced house – one room up, one room down and lean-to kitchen – is not really mine? I rush to the 1960 diary only to find that on January the first, my Uncle Trefor is still reporting that Mr Jenkins has advised him not to offer anyone the rent until it's demanded, but to keep the house in a good state of repair.

I'm too bloody agitated to read through the accounts of Sunday sermons and quarry blastings after that.

And it's that afternoon that the Reverend comes to call, the Reverend Dilwyn Owen, Bethel, a short, fat, jolly-looking man, about sixty years of age. 'I've given you plenty of time to settle in,' he says at the door, smiling a lot.

'I'm not one of the saved,' I tell him. 'I'm a big, bad sinner,

I'm afraid. An alcoholic, for one thing.' Even as I say it, I realize it's not strictly true. I've hardly had a single drink in the last three months and when I went to The Bell last Friday night I only had two halves.

'Then you need friends,' he says.

I give him some brownie points for that. The holy joes usually say they'll fuckin' pray for me. 'Come in.' He's the first person to cross the threshold.

'It's a tidy little cottage,' he says. 'Mr Roberts always kept it nice and you the same.'

'You knew him well? The old man?'

'No one knew him well, but I knew him as well as anyone, I think.'

'Sit down,' I said, pointing to Uncle Trefor's armchair. 'Will you have a cup of tea?' Three months in this place and I'm offering cups of tea to elderly men in dog collars.

'I'll sit and talk, anyhow. I had a cup of tea half an hour ago. I'm getting fat on religious tea.'

'I want to ask you something. Only it's not to do with God.'

'Fire away. It's the God questions I'm frightened of.'

'Did my uncle really own this house? I've been reading his diaries and it seems to me that his landlord's cousins are the real owners.'

'I can put your mind at rest about that. Mr Roberts owned this house. The court granted him the title deeds because he'd maintained it in good order and repair for over twenty years.'

'And that's legal?'

'Perfectly legal. I've got the facts at my fingertips because I often use it as a text for my sermons. It has a great moral significance in my opinion, who owns Wales, for instance, who are the rightful inheritors. But I won't bore you with politics. Suffice it to say, you own this house.'

'I'm very grateful to you. It saves me a trip to Caernarfon and a lot of worry.'

'There we are. What are friends for? Incidentally, do you know what Mr Roberts did with his rent money every week?'

'Used it to maintain the property, you said.'

'He did maintain the property, certainly, but that ten shillings rent he used to send to your mother every week.'

'I remember it arriving every week like clockwork. Ever after that time he came to visit us.'

'Do you know why he visited her? At that time? The only time he ever went further than Caernarfon?

'No. Do you?'

'He'd read in a Sunday newspaper, *The News of the World* it might have been, that your stepfather had been murdered by some drunken fellows outside a local public house and he thought he should find out how your poor mother was taking it.'

'How she was taking it? Do you want the truth? She was over the bloody moon about it. And so was I. And so were all his bloody mates. Sorry about the lingo, Reverend.'

'Your stepfather wasn't a popular character?'

'He was a petty crook, a drunkard, a wife beater and a child molester.'

'He molested you?'

'Yes. He molested me.'

'I think I'll have that cup of tea. Thank you.'

Why shouldn't I tell the Reverend the truth? Let him know something about the real world out there? Yes, I was sexually abused, Reverend, from the age of – what? Three or four? And this at a time when social workers and their like weren't on the lookout for signs of it. No, I never told my mother. Not because I thought she'd turn against me or stop loving me, but because he told me he'd kill me if I did.

Oh, I remember the way he'd kneel over me, pushing his fingers into me front and back, pretending it was fun and that I was supposed to laugh. 'I'm tickling you,' he used to say. And then he'd get his big prick out and hurt me real bad and when I cried he'd say, 'Tell her and I'll kill you.' And when he got his trousers back on, he'd take a knife out of his pocket and stand over me, stroking the blade of it.

I was nine or ten when he was killed. Some neighbours from the estate and the pub got up a collection for my Mum and the day after the funeral we went on the train to a fairground at West Kirby and we went on the Big Dipper over and over again until all the money was gone, shouting out with terror and joy. I didn't tell that bit to the Reverend, but that's what we did. Joy, joy, joy.

My Mum was a big woman like me. She was around forty by this time and she drank a lot and had lots of men friends, but we had quite a good sort of life for the next ten years. Lots of rows and shouting, specially when I got to be thirteen, fourteen, and wanting my own way about everything, but lots of fun and rowdy parties and really great celebrations for birthdays and Christmas.

She died at fifty – cancer – and after that I took over where she left off, work at the factory Monday to Friday and boozing and men at the weekend. And all the men were rough and greedy and easy to hate. There was no way I could admire or love a man was there? The memories of being used and abused stay with you.

The bloody diaries seem to be all I've got. After the quarry shut down, he often left his weeks completely blank except for the Sunday sermons, always Bs. Then in 1986 he starts to write a chirpy little slogan for every week which shows he's softening up but they stop abruptly in February 1987. In fact the diary stops altogether in May 1987. I wonder if he went blind? Or lost his marbles? Who looked after him from 1987 until he died in March this year? Would Netta Morris be likely to tell me? Probably not.

On Friday I go to the corner shop for my groceries. 'This is the tea Mr Roberts liked,' the woman behind the counter tells me.

So she knows who I am. Nosey cow.

I ignored her and bought a different brand. But then I relented. 'Did you know him well?' I asked her. 'He was my great-uncle, but I only met him once.'

'He was a very private man. Didn't speak much to anyone.'

'Who looked after him at the end?'

'He was active to the last, chopping firewood, digging his garden, doing his shopping, chapel of course every Sunday. Didn't smoke or drink. Not much of a life. Wouldn't do for me, I can tell you.'

I looked at her with new interest. 'Didn't I see you in The Bell last week?'

'That's right. My girl-friend and I were hoping you might join us but you left without as much as a glance our way.'

'Will you be there tonight?'

'We're there most nights.'

'See you tonight, then.'

'See you tonight. By the way, do you play darts?'

'Only when I'm sober.'

'Ta-ra then. See you tonight.'

Things are looking up around here. My new friend seems lively enough. Perhaps she'll introduce me to some decent man and a whole new decent way of life. Huh! Perhaps we'll have a few jars and a laugh together anyway.

'You got a husband?' I ask her.

'Yeh, we don't get on. You?'

'No, I don't have that grief. Any kids?'

'Three.'

'I got three kids too. They took them away from me though. They're in this home in Moorfields.'

'That's awful. How did that happen, then?'

'Couldn't stop drinking, that was my trouble.'

'Gets you like that sometimes.'

'Got me like that. Couldn't stop it. Seem to have snapped out of it now, though. Practically on the wagon.'

'You've got something behind you now. Nice little house. Makes all the difference. Try and get them back.'

'I think about it. But I don't know. They've been back that many times. No one believes in me any more.'

'I believe in you, kid. I know how hard it is. There's lots around here know how hard it is, coping with life with next to nothing coming in.'

'I had a good job once.'

'They're wanting chambermaids in the Maesgwyn Arms. That's a good job.'

'I've got no references, though. Nothing up to date.'

'You won't need them. Just tell them who you are. Mr Trefor Roberts's great-niece. Everybody knew him. You've got it made. When you've got a job and a house, you'll get them kids back. How old are they?'

'The girl's fifteen, two boys, nine and eight. The girl's a bit of a problem, though, one way or another.'

'Course she is. So's mine. Mine's sixteen and she was a proper little tearaway. But now she's got a job up Llandudno way, country house hotel, living in, and she comes home on her day off, sunny as you like. You go and see about the job. Things will work out for you in this place, you mark my words. Have another drink.'

'Just one more then.'

The next morning I have a hell of a hangover and I'm

quite pleased about it too. I had a good night out with a new friend and things seem brighter. Maybe I'll go to the Maesgwyn Arms and maybe they'll give me a job on account of my uncle's famed respectability and maybe I'll contact the authorities and maybe I'll get my kids back and maybe we'll manage, as he did, keeping things in good order and repair. For years and years and years. Being bored and bored and bored. Is that all there is to life? I'll have to ask the Reverend. I don't think he'll fob me off with fairy tales. I don't want to be respectable, Reverend, just half-way decent.

Netta Morris knocks at my door. 'You woke me up coming in so late last night,' she says, 'and all that noise. Your uncle never disturbed me in fifty years.'

'Pity he didn't disturb you a bit. I bet you were a good-looking lass fifty years ago.'

'You mind your own business.'

'You want a cup of tea?'

She thinks about it crossly and then comes in. 'Your uncle never asked me in fifty years,' she says.

'Silly old sod,' I say.

Mountain Air

My mother was always happy when she was with her sister, my Auntie Phyllis; she seemed younger too, and much more fun. She and my Auntie Phyllis talked about the time when they were girls, and the world, then, seemed a much brighter place. Their father was a builder with his own business, there was money to spend and he enjoyed spending it, particularly on his pretty daughters.

'Of course we left school at fourteen,' my mother would say. 'I suppose he should have sent us to the County.'

'Whatever for? I was happy enough in my job, weren't you?'

'I suppose so. But I would have liked . . .'

'Of course you were. We never paid a penny for our keep, we always had money for clothes, and what we couldn't afford we could wheedle out of him. Oh, we had a grand time, dancing every Saturday night, the tennis club, the operatic society. Do you remember *The Gondoliers*? Do you remember how many encores we had for 'Three Little Maids from School'?'

I loved it when they got up and put their arms on each other's shoulders and started dancing and singing. They were both plump, my Auntie Phyllis very plump.

'I'm out of condition, Katie,' she'd say at last. 'Just look at me. A stone and a half surplus.'

'Ah, but it's in all the right places,' my mother would reply, planting her hands firmly on her sister's bountiful hips. And they'd both laugh again.

I loved hearing about all the films they'd seen. 'They

knew how to make films those days, a real good story, none of this fancy stuff.' Sometimes one would start unravelling the intricacies of the plot, the other would interrupt her and carry on, but somehow they never got to the end. 'Do you remember the woman in the one-and-nines who was forever turning round to tell us what was coming next? She used to go to the pictures every night of the week and sometimes the Saturday matinée as well. She smelt of mothballs. Her face was dead white. Someone said she put flour on it.' 'She was a nice old thing, though. She sometimes gave us mintoes.' 'They tasted of mothballs.' 'Didn't we laugh?'

Most of their anecdotes ended like that. 'Didn't we laugh?' They'd had some good times.

I knew everything about their lives when they were young; their adventures with Will Jenkins, bus conductor, and Charlie Smith, commercial traveller, the wonderful summer when they'd had a college student each. 'From Aber they were, and doing Teacher Training in the County. We met them in the clubhouse, didn't we Katie, and right from the start Jim Parry fancied you and Bob Howells fancied me.' She sighed. 'So often it worked out wrong, the one I liked, liked you, the one you liked, liked me, but that time we were all happy. Do you remember that handsome park-attendant we met at one of the summer concerts? The one with the shoulders? What was his name? Ken something, if I remember right. But do you remember that little runt he brought along with him the next Saturday? Which one of us was he meant for, I wonder? We just drank our shandies and disappeared round the back.'

'Ken Williams,' my mother said, with a touch of sadness, 'Ken Williams. That was his name.'

I felt sure he'd liked her best. It was in her voice.

I often wondered how they'd ended up with my Uncle

Jack and my father; my father an insurance collector with very little sense of humour and my Uncle Jack a small-time painter and decorator who drank too much.

I suppose I was the only one who paid any attention to their reminiscences. They had eight children between them, four each, but I was the only girl. The boys liked to be out kicking a ball whenever they got together; except for Bobby, Auntie Phyllis's youngest, who was still a baby.

We didn't get to see each other very often, but every year in the summer holidays we had a day out in the mountains. Our family lived in the town so that we had further to travel, my Auntie Phyllis's family lived in a village nine miles up the valley so they were almost half-way there.

The trip took a lot of organization. Neither family had a phone, so that arrangements like, 'the first fine day next week,' were fraught with suspense and danger. A day which began cloudy or even rainy might clear up in a few hours, but would Auntie Phyllis have listened to the forecast?

I loved the bus journey up the valley, between gentle meadows and little wooded hills, but couldn't settle to be happy until I saw the other family waiting in Pontgoch. Yes, there they were, Michael and the twins out in the middle of the road, waving their bags at the driver, in case he shouldn't notice my very plump auntie and Bobby flagging him down at the bus-stop. (I loved my cousin Michael, but he didn't take much notice of me because he was so much older; big and tall and stern-looking.)

Other passengers would move to other seats so that we could all sit together, congratulating one another on the cloudless sky and comparing picnic food. 'I've got corned beef sandwiches for dinner, ham sandwiches for tea, four packets of custard creams and four bottles of pop,' my Auntie Phyllis would say. She always had white bread and butter and lovely shop jam, while my mother had brown bread, home-made jam and home-made cake. Our food was left till last.

I took Bobby on my lap. The others could go off and do whatever stupid things they chose as long as I had Bobby. 'Can I carry him? Can I carry him?' I begged, as soon as we got off the bus.

'No, let him walk a little way, Megan. You shall give him a piggy-back when he's tired.'

'Upp-a. Upp-a.' Bobby said, holding out little fat arms, and of course I hoisted him up there and then.

The mountains were lovely, green and round-backed, the heat-haze just lifting. 'Well, here we are,' my Auntie Phyllis always said as soon as we'd walked a few yards from the road. 'This is Wales, isn't it boys. This is where we belong.'

'When I leave school I'm going to Birmingham,' Ifor, one of the twins said. 'Aston Villa for ever!'

'Give us a song, Gareth,' my mother said quickly. The smaller of the twins had a prize-winning treble voice.

'Give us a song, choirboy,' the other boys chanted.

'Now don't start fighting till you've put your bags down. I don't want any broken bottles. Remember last year.'

At last we reached the ideal picnic spot; the ground almost flat, large boulders for back-rests, a trickling stream, not too many sheep droppings and the road still visible, a winding silver thread far below us; my mother liked to be in sight of the road.

I think I must have been eight or nine the year we missed the bus back; my brothers and cousins all in their teens except for Bobby, nearly two.

We ate and drank soon after midday and after a story-telling contest which my eldest brother won, the big boys ran off to explore and I was left to play with Bobby.

He was a good-natured, contented baby, very easy to

amuse. I only had to put one of his little toys on my head and tip it off and he'd laugh as though it was the greatest trick in the world. I suppose I carried on doing that for half an hour. Afterwards I recited nursery rhymes, tickled his little fat belly, kissed and cuddled him until at last he fell asleep and Auntie Phyllis laid him down in the cropped grass with her cardigan over him.

'Are you going to find the boys now?' she asked me.

'No, I've got a book to read.'

'Aren't you a clever one. Not one of mine has ever read a book. Not from choice, anyhow.'

I opened my library book, but only pretended to read. It was much more interesting to listen to the conversation going on behind me. My mother and Auntie Phyllis weren't speaking now about the golden days when they were young, but about their present lives. They spoke softly, almost in whispers at times, but I could follow most of it. I kept my eyes on my book, but my ears attuned to them.

Perhaps they suspected that I was eavesdropping; Auntie Phyllis referred to Uncle Jack as Mr Plum and my mother called my father the Reverend.

'Have I told you about the time Mr Plum stayed out till stop-tap and his poor wife put his supper down in front of him, telling him off a bit, I daresay, and what did he do but turn his plate head over tip onto the clean tablecloth and get himself some bread and cheese. "Take that away," he said to his wife after. "Clear that up." "Not on your life," she said. "There it stays as far as I'm concerned and if you don't take it away, there it'll be for your children to see in the morning." '

'What happened?' my mother asked, a thrill of fear in her voice.

'The poor woman went to bed eventually and when he came up at last he said in a low voice, yes, he had cleared it up. "And did you rinse out the cloth?" she asked him. "Did I hell," he said and with that he cracked his shin against the side of the bed and went hopping about on one leg, making such a to-do that she couldn't help laughing at him. And in the end he started to laugh too, and that was the end of that.'

'The Reverend is so tight-fisted, Phyllis. His poor wife has to account for every penny. You wouldn't believe how she's got to scrimp and save before the family can have any little treat. Every week he has to have something put by for the children's education. I suppose he means well and it might be worth it in the end, but meanwhile his poor wife can't afford to have her shoes mended. Never a penny for any new clothes.'

'At least he doesn't drink, Katie.'

'He's too mean to drink, girl. Too mean to have any vices.'

'Mr Plum's got plenty. One of them works behind the bar of the Red Lion.'

'You don't mean it.'

'Cross my heart. A common piece, too, big mouth and a skirt up to her crotch. His wife goes in there with him the occasional Friday night. When she pulls the beer, she leans towards him showing everything she's got. On his birthday, when his sisters were down that time and they all went in for a drink, her behind the bar gave him such a long birthday kiss, everyone was counting and banging the bar and cheering.'

'Whatever did his wife do?'

'Pretended to laugh like everybody else. But the next morning when the pub opened she went along to have a quiet word. Only the little tart was in her rollers with no make-up on and she felt sorry for her somehow. So she said she'd come in to ask whether they'd found her scarf, and they both searched for it, best of friends. And the next night he said, "I didn't know you'd lost your scarf, kid." "Who told you I had?" "Kim, the girl behind the bar." "And I suppose Kim is your little bit on the side?" she asks him. "Does a man need a little bit on the side when he's got a gorgeous piece like you at home?" he says, slapping her bottom.'

'At least they have their bit of fun. Mr Plum has his faults, yes, but I bet he gives his wife some good times. The Reverend is much too virtuous to enjoy himself, even going for a walk on a Sunday afternoon is wearing out shoe leather. Do you know when his poor wife last went to the pictures? Can you guess when she last had a holiday? Her father, God rest his soul, warned her that he was a dry old stick. Never trust a man in a dicky-bow, he used to say, and never trust a man with no faults.'

I didn't understand everything they said by a long way, but I got the gist of it; life wasn't easy even when you were grown-up – not if you were a woman anyhow. I sighed and turned over on my belly and started to count my afflictions: straight hair, freckles, not much good at sums, hopeless at rounders. And a girl as well.

I fell asleep.

When I woke up, Bobby was whining and my mother and my Auntie Phyllis were in a state about something and taking no notice of him. 'What's the matter?' I asked them.

'Give him a drop of lemonade, Megan,' Auntie Phyllis said. 'That's right, and jig him up and down a bit, he's always fretful when he's slept too long.'

'What time is it?'

'Gone half past four, love, and those good-for-nothing lads not back for their tea. Quarter to four, I said, didn't I Katie? Don't be later than a quarter to four, I said over and over again. The bus goes at five past five and it's the only one. What if we miss it? We'd have to hire a car from somewhere and what about the expense? Michael would have to walk back to that hotel on the road to Tregroes and ask if he could use their phone.'

'I don't know what Meurig will say if we don't use our return tickets. He can't bear waste.'

'What's happened to them, that's what I'd like to know. They've never been late before, you know that. They're usually back before they've gone, their tongues hanging out for the rest of the lemonade.'

'Can I give Bobby some biscuits?'

'Yes, love, and have some yourself. There's some sandwiches too. Strawberry jam. Oh, what's happened to our children? Thank goodness we've got one each left, Katie. Do you feel like having a little run up to the brow of that hill, Megan, to see if you can catch a glimpse of them?'

'No, Phyllis, she's not to. As soon as you get to the top of one, there's another and another. I don't want her getting lost as well.'

'Well, what if we leave them here to find their own way back? What's a ten-mile trek to healthy youngsters? Six of them together, they'd have a great time. I could put yours to sleep with mine and send them back on the ten-fifteen tomorrow. Their tickets would probably be all right.'

'We . . . we can't leave them,' I said, bursting into tears.

'If we think about something else, they'll turn up,' my mother said. 'Let's have a game of I-Spy.'

'I spy with my little eye . . . Oh, don't be silly Katie. Look, why don't you three start walking down towards the road, I'll wait here to hurry them up when they arrive and you ask the bus driver to hang on a bit.'

'They've got to run according to the timetable, Phyllis. He wouldn't wait.'

'He'd wait five or ten minutes if you asked him nicely. He knows it's the last bus.' By this time, my Auntie Phyllis was morosely eating her way through the jam sandwiches.

'I'm ten years too old to ask him nicely.'

'No you're not. You flutter those eyelashes and let your mouth quiver a bit. You as well, Megan. You've got to learn sometime. Right, let's have a little rehearsal.'

'Let's all shout,' my mother suggested. 'If we all shout together perhaps they'll hear us.'

'What shall we shout?'

'Ice-cream. That would bring them.'

'Issceam,' Bobby said, spitting out his biscuit.

'Ice-cream', we shouted. 'Ice-cream. Ice-cream.'

'Now we've frightened those sheep. What a noise. Oh, let's all start walking down. Thank goodness most of the bags are empty. I'll take Bobby, Megan. In case you fall, love.'

We scrambled and stumbled down the side of the mountain, looking behind us every few minutes, feeling uneasy. It had become chilly. Clouds scurried by, casting their shadows over us. The mountains seemed full of menace.

We were still quite a distance from the road when we saw the bus passing by. To others it might seem a friendly old thing; a top speed of thirty miles an hour and noisy on the gear change, to us it was treacherous as a tiger. My mother sat down on a mossy stone, white with worry.

'Where are those sinners?' my Auntie Phyllis asked.

'Meurig will be meeting the bus,' my mother said. 'What will he have for his supper? I'd got him a nice piece of haddock, but I know he won't cook it himself.'

'He can get some fish and chips for once.'

'Oh, he won't do that Phyllis. Not after giving me the week's housekeeping.'

'Anyway it's those damned boys you should be worrying about. Meurig is safe enough.'

'Issceam,' Bobby shouted, waving back at where a posse of boys were whooping down the mountain.

Michael reached us first and my Auntie Phyllis clouted him round the head. 'We've missed the bloody bus,' she said. 'Where have you all been?'

'It's alright,' he said, rubbing his ear. 'We've been helping a farmer and he's going to bring his van and give us all a lift back.'

'Is he?' my mother asked. 'Is he really?' Oh, that's something Phyllis, isn't it? But what have you been doing? We brought you up here for a day out on the mountains, not to help farmers.'

'There was a sheep got out on a ledge,' one of my brothers said. 'Been out there since Sunday, the farmer told us. And he was trying to get her back. But it was too dangerous for him to get down the ledge to get a rope round her. But Gareth did it.'

'Gareth did it?' my Auntie Phyllis screamed, shaking him and clouting him soundly.

'He's the smallest of us, Auntie, so there was less chance of him dislodging the stones.'

Gareth moved a judicious few yards from his mother. 'And I put the rope round her belly and tied it tight and then Mr Llywellyn and the boys hauled her up and after they got her safe, they threw the rope down to me and hauled me up.'

'Oh my Lord. You wait till your father hears about this. You risked your life. We bring you up here for a day out in the mountain air and you decide to go risking life and limb. What if you'd fallen down onto another ledge and been stuck there all night? Oh my Lord. What would poor Ifor have done if you'd been killed?'

'I'd have been OK,' Ifor said, at which my Auntie Phyllis lunged out and clouted him too.

'She breathed all over my face,' Gareth said. 'She knew I was rescuing her. She kept looking at me. Her eyes never blinked and her breath was hot as flame. She kept looking at me and breathing.'

'They're all safe, thank Heavens,' my mother said. 'And I suppose Gareth was very brave, even though he shouldn't have done it. Put your mother first, Gareth, in future. Doesn't your mother mean more to you than a sheep?'

'When is this man coming to fetch us?' my Auntie Phyllis asked, since Gareth seemed in no hurry to reply.

'He can't come till six because of the milking, but he's got a big van, he says, with plenty of room for us all.'

'And are you sure he'll come, Michael?' my mother asked. 'Do you trust him?'

Michael looked at her steadily. 'I do, Auntie. I trust him.'

Suddenly the tension lifted and the spell of the mountains was on us again. We had almost an hour to wait, but who cared. It was getting cold now, but we could still feel the sun-glow on our bodies and there were three packets of biscuits left and a full bottle of lemonade.

Gareth came out of his sulks and sang 'Yr Arglwydd Iôr', and 'Oh, for the Wings of a Dove', and then in the spotlight of the westering sun with the lovely mountains, blue and violet, as backdrop, my mother and my Auntie Phyllis went through their considerable repertoire of songs and dances.

Mr Llywellyn arrived soon after six and though my Auntie Phyllis had sworn to speak her mind to him about the danger to Gareth, she changed her mind when she found how concerned he was that we'd missed our bus, how apologetic about the goings-on of sheep, 'as okkard as women,' he said they were, and in no time she was laughing with him and poking him in the ribs.

He gave Gareth a ten-shilling note and all the rest of us, even Bobby, a two-shilling piece.

It was bumpy in the back of the van and you couldn't see out, but I was sitting next to Michael and after a while he showed me how to whistle with a piece of grass between your thumbs. And when at last I managed a little squeak, he said I was a jolly good sport.

When we got home, my father was standing by the empty grate looking very sorry for himself.

'You missed the bus,' he said mournfully. 'However did you get home?'

'We managed fine,' my mother said. 'You worry too much, Meurig, and you work too hard. You should have come with us to the mountains.'

And with that, she put her hands tightly round his waist and danced him round and round and round the spinning kitchen.

Anniversary

Joanna had been worried about inviting Fanny to dinner. 'She's such a strange girl. She's not our type, not really. I don't know what you'll think of her.' She was even more anxious than usual that everything should be just right. 'Is it too extravagant, Paul? You see, I think Fanny's quite hard-up. I don't want her to think I'm trying to impress her.'

'It's perfect,' I said.

It was. Cream linen mats on gleaming mahogany. A simple table setting. A small centrepiece of pale pink roses. The french windows open to the June garden.

'Iced vichyssoise. Sole. Chicken marengo.'

'Perfect.'

'The Grants, us and Fanny.'

'Just right.'

Joanna was looking sun-flushed and pretty. She's a large girl, then she was larger; Simon was only six weeks old, her breasts were heavy and deep. She wore a white dress with brown and violet splashes.

'Don't worry,' I said, patting her shoulder. She smiled abstractedly at me.

I try to remember how I felt about Joanna in that time before Fanny. Fond of her, I suppose, as always. It doesn't change. I've never loved her passionately. Even when I asked her to marry me I realized that, but in a way had more faith in the steadier beating of my heart; I'd already had several love affairs, some painful. Joanna was rich, that made her different too. In those days I was poor. Now I'm successful enough to keep her in the manner to which she's accustomed, rich enough to pay the upkeep of this large house her father gave us as a wedding present.

'I'll slip up to say good-night to Sara and Elizabeth,' Joanna said. Sara was six, then, Elizabeth four.

She was still upstairs when Fanny arrived, a few minutes early.

Joanna had told me that Fanny was our age. 'About thirty,' she had said. She didn't look thirty. She looked like a young girl.

Joanna had met her in the nursing home six weeks before when she was having Simon. Fanny had had a son, too, an illegitimate baby. That's all I'd been told about her. I hadn't been interested in her then.

'I'm Fanny,' she said, holding out her hand, a bony well-shaped hand. Her hair was tawny, her skin brown, her eyes grey.

So this is it, I thought. Love at first sight. Recognition, sharp and immediate. Excitement at the first touch of a cool hand. Desire on a summer night, even before the first drink.

'May I bring him in? Thomas? I've got him in the carry-cot.'

'Of course. Let me carry him. Joanna, here's Fanny.'

'Lovely to see you again,' Joanna said.

'Where shall I put the baby?' I asked.

'On the bed in the guest room. Say good-night to the girls, darling, while you're upstairs. Fanny, do you want to go up to see that Thomas is all right?'

'No, he's fast asleep. Can I give you a hand with anything? What a beautiful house this is. It's lovely to be here.'

I wondered about the almost palpable warmth between Joanna and Fanny as I took the carry-cot into the guest room, checking that the window was open, but not too widely; Joanna isn't usually sympathetic towards unconventional people. I peeped in at Thomas and was rather disconcerted to find his dark eyes wide open. I backed away, closing the door carefully, looked in at the girls and hurried downstairs. I remember so well the lightness, almost giddiness, of heart I felt; the humdrum old world was still full of surprises, perhaps glory.

By the time I got down, the Grants, Mabel and Geoffrey and their undergraduate son, Adam, had arrived. We had drinks on the terrace, Adam bombarding Fanny with heavy undergraduate humour, Mabel and Geoffrey listening and looking on, Joanna pretending to listen, but with her mind in the kitchen, Fanny smiling at Adam, but looking at me from time to time, I out of my depth in love, carried along by the swift and terrible current, uncaring whether I should sink or swim.

Dinner was perfect, as I'd predicted, the food and wine superb, Joanna relaxed and happy. Geoffrey, often pompous and foolish, talking very well and amusingly before a new audience, Adam quietly concentrating on the meal.

I don't think Joanna had told me that Fanny was a writer; perhaps I'd forgotten it. Her latest book, *Death Valley*, a macabre science-fiction, had recently collected some rave reviews. Geoffrey had read it and told us it was first-rate. Mabel thought she might have read it and spent quite a long time describing a different book altogether, Adam egging her on.

'No dear,' Geoffrey said at last.

That's all I remember of the conversation, a taste of *Death Valley*. But I remember Fanny's smile as we talked about it. I remember the way she ate her strawberries. I remember the four or five freckles on her straight, perfect nose. I remember her eyes, grey and luminous.

'You'll take Fanny home, won't you Paul?' Joanna asked me when the Grants had gone.

'Of course.'

'But I've got the car.'

'I'll drive you back and walk home, it'll do me good.'

I remember Joanna waving to us and looking pleased.

I drove Fanny home in her white Mini.

'I hope we'll see a lot more of you,' I said, lifting the carry-cot from the back seat.

'Of course. We're neighbours, aren't we?'

She let herself into the house and held the door open for me.

'Shall I carry him upstairs for you?'

'Please.'

Her tiny house, half a mile down the hill from ours, was built by an architect – a friend of mine – as a weekend retreat. It gives the impression of a child's tree-house.

'He sleeps in here.'

The room was white and bare. I thought of Simon's large nursery, its sunny colours, its mobiles and toys and Peter Rabbit friezes.

'Is he all right? Are you going to feed him?'

She didn't answer. Only looked at him swiftly and closed the door.

'And this is my room,' she said.

Oh, the complications of previous affairs, and the Herculean labours involved in ending up in any empty room with a space on the floor, let alone a crystal white room and a sea-green bed.

It was so easy. We stood in front of the mirror together and smiled at how easy, and how beautiful, it was.

That's how it started. Seven years ago this month. Does Joanna know about it? That causes me a great deal of anxiety. I don't know. She never asks me to take Fanny home now, simply knows I will, knows that I often call in to see her on my way home from the station. Well, everyone accepts that we have a great deal in common, Fanny and I.

Certainly, Joanna and Fanny are still firm friends. They meet for morning coffee and go shopping together. They have dinner together even when I'm away. Simon and Thomas are inseparable; the terrible twins. We're close neighbours.

Occasionally it seems that I've got it all: a rich complacent wife, a beautiful mistress.

There are other times when things seem insupportable.

A few weeks ago Joanna and I were sitting together after dinner watching the sun sinking behind the beeches. For me it seemed such a consoling moment. I'd had a hectic day, a conference, a site meeting, another conference.

'Happy?' I asked.

A dangerous, foolish question. Joanna turned her head away, but not before I'd seen the tears come to her eyes.

'We could be any ordinary couple,' she said.

The resigned sadness in her voice moved me. I'm so fond of her. She's good and kind and placid. Why is it that I've never had a moment's excitement in her presence? Yes, she's physically rather cold, but men have worn their hearts out over cold women often enough. I put my hand on hers, hating myself.

I suppose I married Joanna for her money. Though as I've already said more than once, I was certainly fond of her, felt protective and warm towards her, but I don't think I would have married her if she hadn't been rich.

We met at a party, a smart literary party. She was out of her depth and I looked after her; that was innocent enough, even chivalrous. She came from Leeds, she told me, had studied Domestic Economy at Edinburgh, didn't have a job, wasn't sure that she wanted one. An old school friend, a girl I knew slightly and disliked, had brought her to the party, she knew no one else. She was staying in London only until the next day.

She was a little older than I was, tall, raven-haired, easy on the eye, even though her elaborate dress was out of place amongst the little silky shifts of the Sixties. Something about her moved me, perhaps I'd already sniffed her moneyed background even in ten minutes' talk. Whatever it was, I rescued her from the party, took her to as decent a restaurant as I could afford, then back, by a taxi I remember, to her hotel. I gave her my telephone number and asked her to ring me when she was next in London. I didn't kiss her goodnight. I wanted to. But even more, I wanted her to think me courteous and undemanding. I'd never before wanted to give anyone that impression and wondered if I could have fallen in love.

I walked home in a slightly bemused state. I'd gone to the party to find a girl to sleep with.

Next morning I rang her hotel intending to ask her to have lunch with me, but she had already left.

I'd forgotten about her when she phoned me about a month later. I'd recently got my first job and was working hard.

She invited me to have dinner with her and her parents at their hotel. I tried to get out of it, I was meeting a girl that night and besides, the invitation sounded so dull.

'What about tomorrow night?' she asked then, her voice so forlorn that I remembered in a flash how she had looked at the party; the anxious expression, the tight little smile. It was new to me, the concern I felt. I told her I'd see her the next night.

I wore the suit I'd bought for my new job and arrived punctually.

Her parents were much as I'd imagined; her mother

quiet and over-dressed, her father brash and eager to impress, demanding – and getting – good, plain food, and sending the wine back; and talking about his factory, his men, his overseas commitments, his plans for the future. I enjoyed the unaccustomed luxury of the meal and talked almost as much as he did, about the firm of architects I'd been with for ten days, inventing what I didn't know.

I wondered whether I'd be able to see Joanna alone after the meal, wondered whether I wanted to. She was certainly good-looking, but not my type. All the same, I tried to think of a respectable place I could offer to take her to.

We moved into the lounge for coffee. 'Would you like a walk?' I asked her after about half an hour. 'Just as far as the park perhaps?'

She was beautiful when she smiled.

Her mother was afraid of the rain. 'Oh, the rain won't do them any harm,' her father said. 'They won't melt.'

He approved of me, there was no doubt about that.

Joanna went up to her room to fetch her coat and umbrella and when she had gone, he turned to me. 'Well, we knew she'd be getting a young man sometime; all the same it's not easy for us. She's all we've got, you know.'

'We'll be back in ten minutes,' I said, my head reeling with the knowledge that I'd been so readily accepted as their daughter's young man, her future husband if I decided on it. Wouldn't you think, I asked myself, that a man in his position would have a short-list of suitable applicants for his only daughter's hand? Why me? What had she told them about me?

Before I took her back to the hotel, I kissed her. In spite of the umbrella, her face was cold and wet. I kissed her eyes and her lips. Kissing gave me a proud feeling, like doing well in an examination.

I saw her every night that week and when she went back

to Leeds I wrote to her and telephoned as though I was really her young man. I was invited to her home for Christmas. We got engaged on Boxing Day. I was twenty-two, she was two years older.

I shouldn't have married her, I suppose. I should have resisted the appeal in her eyes; it was certainly there. From the beginning I was aware that she wanted me, planned to marry me.

I wasn't sure why, but came to the conclusion that I was simply different in some way from the men she was used to meeting.

'Why did you decide on me?' I ask her sometimes.

She manages to smile and look pained at the same time.

'Didn't you do even a bit of deciding?' she asks me.

'Of course I did.'

It's there even now, the gentle vulnerability which took the place of excitement.

The first year of our marriage was the worst. I wasn't even careful enough to hide my miserable affairs.

After Sara was born, I made a conscious effort to be faithful. Fatherhood steadied me. I found Sara enchanting and used to rush home to see her. Joanna seemed fulfilled and relaxed and I was no longer angry about what I'd let myself drift into. No wonder we had a second baby so soon. I'm a devoted father. I used to bath them and tell bedtime stories and get up in the night. Joanna thought I was a reformed character. Not that she had ever complained before; not even when I had stayed in town all night or when I got a phone call in the early hours.

We limped along without serious mishaps for three or four years.

I'm quite pleased to remember that when Fanny took me into her life, I was on the brink of an affair with a young girl from the typing pool. I try to tell myself how much more disastrous that would have been; a young self-centred girl snatching at my evenings and keeping me from my family.

Fanny saved me from those complications. Our sexual life is well-regulated and fits into my domestic pattern. I drop in to see her on my way home from the station. 'I called in on Fanny as I came past,' I tell Joanna afterwards. 'She may come up later.'

Nowadays, with Thomas and Simon still up and about, it's more difficult, but even snatched minutes in the locked study are more important to me than anything else in my life.

For I love her obsessively. Every pretty young girl reminds me of her. The nape of someone's neck, someone's round elbow, and I am stung again by the bitterness of loving her. She is so self-contained that my love seems pitiful. She doesn't need my love.

What does she need except herself and her small, dark son, her tiny house, and her garden dug out of the side of the hill?

Sometimes I ring her before I leave the office. 'Shall I call in tonight?' I have thought about her all day long.

'By all means. Unless you're busy. Are you entertaining? Are you bringing work home?'

She's so understanding. So cool.

I go in and she pours me a drink. 'But I thought you were going straight home tonight.'

'I didn't say that.'

'That's what I understood. Wasn't that why you rang?'

'I rang hoping you'd ask me to call.'

'I don't want to start making demands on you. You should know that.'

I long for her so fiercely that I would welcome any demands, however unreasonable. If she said, Don't go home tonight. Phone Joanna and tell her you're staying

with me, that's what I would do, I know it. But I also know
that she would never ask it.

'If I were free, Fanny, would you marry me?'

'No, I don't want marriage. Once was enough.'

'What do you want?'

'Freedom. Time to write. Nice moments. Friends. Thomas.'

'Was Thomas a mistake?'

'Certainly not.'

'You planned to have a child?'

'That's right.'

'Why?'

'Why not? I'm not rich, but I have enough money. I wanted
a child.'

'Who is his father?'

'Why do you ask? My ex-husband.'

'But you were divorced from him long before Thomas
was conceived.'

'That's right. But we went on seeing each other from time
to time. We're not enemies. I told him I wanted a child.'

'And he obliged you?'

'Why do you find it offensive? We were married once,
that should make it better rather than worse.'

'Did you hope it might lead to remarriage?'

'No. He is remarried. Very happily. He has four children.
That's why I knew he wouldn't want a share of Thomas. It
seemed an excellent arrangement. Why are you so jealous,
Paul? Aren't you happy with me?'

I can never stop questioning her, however many times I
resolve not to do so.

'How long were you married?'

'Three years.'

'How old were you when you got married?'

'Twenty.'

'Was he your first lover?'

'Yes.'

'Was he handsome?'

'Yes. Not as handsome as you, but he was well enough.'

'Was he kind to you?'

'Sometimes.'

'Were you unhappy? When you decided to part?'

'Of course I was unhappy.'

Why can't she lie to me, or refuse to answer? I question her until I'm too tormented to go on.

I draw her to me, trying to make her feel my wretchedness as I kiss and leave her. I realize that we are not alike in anything but in our disloyalty to Joanna, and our amorality: she is not in love.

'How was Fanny?' Joanna asks later.

'Exasperating as ever.'

That's the role we play in public, friends baiting each other, lightly disagreeing on every subject. Perhaps even Joanna believes in it.

Perhaps I shouldn't remain with Joanna feeling as I do about Fanny. But would it be kinder if I left her? I don't know. I'm very fond of her and of my children.

Although no one else is aware of the fact, it is exactly seven years since Fanny first came to visit us. Once again the Grants, at my suggestion, are coming to dinner; they now live in London, we don't see them as often as we did, and Fanny has also been invited. I wonder if I shall tell her later on that I am celebrating seven years of pleasure and torment. Probably not. This summer I have a premonition that we are at some danger point and am chary of precipitating a crisis.

It is a Saturday. We have lunch in the garden. Simon is in disgrace for putting a snail in Elizabeth's salad. Joanna, Sara and Elizabeth beg me to spank him; I look at him fiercely and they all beg me not to – I wasn't going to anyway – but he, probably a tiny bit scared, blurts out, 'Fanny and Thomas have gone to Manchester.'

'Fanny and Thomas have gone to Manchester have they?' I manage to say. 'Fanny and Thomas have gone to Manchester, so that gives you an excuse, does it, for upsetting your mother in this horrid way. Well, you'll have no strawberries, not one. Go and sit over there till we've finished, then you can help Mrs Leigh clear the table.'

Fanny and Thomas have gone to Manchester. My outrage at this trip I hadn't been told about causes me to deal too severely with poor Simon; I can see that he's near to tears. Elizabeth, a little ashamed of the fuss she's made, picks up the snail, now gently perambulating along the tablecloth, puts it in the nearest flower bed and returns to eat a little of her cold meat.

Afterwards I share out the strawberries – between four – we eat them joylessly. 'He deserves a lesson,' Joanna says. 'He and Thomas are getting quite out of control.'

After my coffee, I phone Fanny's number, but she has already left. Why has she gone to Manchester when she'd promised to have dinner with us? I can't bring myself to question Simon who is still looking reproachfully at me.

It isn't that I expect to be consulted about all her movements. She never tells me, for instance, when she has a day in London. Quite often I only learn that she is out for the evening when Joanna asks me to baby-sit for her. 'She's gone to the theatre,' Joanna says. 'Who is she with? What is she seeing?' 'I didn't ask her, darling. does it matter?'

In the afternoon, Elizabeth goes to a birthday party. It's one of the drawbacks of the Thames Valley affluent society that one or other of the children is invited to a birthday party almost every Saturday afternoon, which means that the other two have to be taken out for a treat. This afternoon Sara and Simon, Joanna and I and several thousand other

people visit a stately home and an adventure playground.
We're late picking up Elizabeth which embarrasses Joanna,
and all the time I'm wondering why Fanny has gone to
Manchester without telling me and how I can tolerate a
whole Saturday, perhaps a whole weekend, without seeing
her.

'Will Thomas be back tomorrow?' I ask Simon later, when
he comes in to say goodnight.

'Oh no. He's gone for a long time.'

I can't believe it. 'For a weekend?' I suggest.

'Oh no, for a long time. Perhaps for ever.' That's as much
help as I'm going to have from Simon.

Geoffrey and Mabel are late. They blame the Saturday
crowds on the road, but I suspect that they've been lingering
in a pub.

Mabel has recently had a small operation and gives us
many details we'd rather be spared.

Geoffrey asks after Fanny, who usually comes up whenever
they visit us. 'She's gone to Manchester,' I say, trying to
keep some of the bitterness out of my voice. 'At least, so
Simon tells us. We're not informed of her plans.'

'Manchester, eh.' Geoffrey says. 'I wonder if she's seeing
Adam.'

'Why ever should she be seeing Adam?' Mabel says
sharply. 'In a city of over half a million people, the chances
are that she could be seeing someone else.'

I'd completely forgotten that Adam was in Manchester.
A hard lump rises into my throat.

'Mabel can't bear to think that Adam is interested in
Fanny, can you?'

'I'm very fond of Fanny, you know that; there's absolutely
no one I'm fonder of. All the same, I think she's too old for
Adam, I admit it. After all Joanna, she's seven or eight
years older than Adam, isn't she?'

'I didn't know there was anything at all between them,' Joanna says. 'I didn't realize they ever saw each other.'

'They see each other,' Geoffrey says.

'They simply lunch together occasionally when he's home,' Mabel says. 'That's all. She amuses him. You know how amusing she can be.'

I have to see to the wine so I'm able to keep out of the conversation and contemplate just how amusing Fanny can be and how I would like to wring her amusing little neck.

'Adam adores her books. He's got every one of them,' Mabel says. 'He has an intellectual interest in her. Nothing more than that.'

I hadn't seen Adam for quite some time and considered myself lucky on that score. Now I was forced to turn my thoughts to him. Apparently he had been promoted to the post of director's assistant on some weekly television programme. Mabel has actually seen him at work in the studio, and spends some time telling us about it. Geoffrey, realizing that we're probably not anxious to spend the entire meal hearing about boom microphones and tracking cameras, keeps trying to cut in, while Joanna says 'Really,' and 'How interesting,' and I'm free to think my murderous thoughts.

She can't be seeing Adam, she can't be. Why not? He's young, fairly handsome, drives a sports car, has an interesting job. He's a stupid ass, that's why not. A boring and pompous ass, that's why not. She can't be seeing Adam Grant. She would have told me something about it. Would she? Has she ever told me anything about the lunches they've had together? Does she give me any information except if I plague her for it, drag it out of her, word by word?

'Of course, Mabel wants him to marry some pure young girl,' Geoffrey says. 'But are there any these days? He'd have to marry her straight from school or even earlier. I was sitting next to a couple of young girls in the Tube one morning last week and you simply wouldn't believe what they were talking about. They looked about sixteen, not much more. You simply wouldn't believe what they were talking about. And not keeping their voices down either. Well, I'm not easily embarrassed, you know me. After six years in the navy, a chap isn't easily embarrassed, but I tell you I was hot under the collar.'

'Do tell us what they were saying, dear,' Mabel says. 'After this amount of lead-in, I think we deserve to hear. Oh, Geoffrey, do you remember that dinner party when I kept talking to Sir Donald about my vulva instead of my Volvo. No wonder we haven't seen him since.'

'No, the reason I approve of Adam seeing Fanny is that she might save him from a disastrous emotional entanglement. I don't want to think that he'll fall in love and rush into marriage before he's had time to enjoy himself. He's safe with Fanny. I don't think a man is mature enough for marriage until he's thirty.'

'Paul was twenty-two when we got married,' Joanna says, giving me a small, sad smile.

'And Geoffrey was twenty-four,' Mabel says brightly. 'But of course he's an exceptional man who matured early. Aren't you darling? Aren't you exceptional?'

'Fanny is modern in the way that you two aren't, thank God,' Geoffrey goes on in his most pontifical manner. 'She's completely independent, self-reliant, coolly self-aware. She enjoys sex in a casual way and is determined not to be swamped by any nonsense like falling in love. It wouldn't surprise me if she'd had her little boy, what's his name? Thomas? By artificial insemination. Do you know what I mean? So that he'd be entirely hers.'

Suddenly, I can't bear another word. It isn't what he's saying, most of which is probably true, but the way he's assuming a special knowledge of her, a special intimacy with her. I can't bear it.

'She's not so detached as you think,' I say, all the authority of love and brandy in my voice. 'She got married when she was twenty. Fanny got married when she was twenty,' – so much was true – 'she was a beautiful, inexperienced girl tumultuously in love.' I could see her before me, candid of eye and beautiful, as I spoke. 'Her husband was quite a bit older than she was, a professional musician, Anton or some such phoney name, with no shortage of girlfriends. After a time Fanny could take no more and she threatened to divorce him and to her dismay, he did nothing to deter her. The divorce went through. She was heart-broken. She's never got over it.'

Geoffrey and Mabel look at me in stunned silence. Geoffrey is the first to rally.

'I hope you haven't told us too much, old boy,' he says, genuine concern in his voice. 'You haven't been too free with the confidential stuff, have you? Anyway, we'll keep it to ourselves, won't we Mabel? Absolutely. Poor little Fanny. What a brave front she puts on it. Well, well, well. Can you ever know anyone? What secrets are you hiding from us, Mabel? Joanna? Life isn't what it seems, it certainly isn't.'

Mabel is silent and grave, but at the same time probably relieved on Adam's account. As for me, I am completely desolate, certain somehow that what I spoke so rashly and brazenly was the truth. My brain, like a computer, has processed all the bits and pieces of information which I've extracted from Fanny over seven years of close questioning and come up with the answer.

'I must keep some pavlova for Simon,' I hear Joanna say. 'He was so upset about Thomas going away that he behaved rather badly during lunch and Paul wouldn't let him have any strawberries.'

'I didn't know Fanny had told you about Anton,' Joanna says as we're getting ready for bed that night.

I make a non-committal sound. So I was right. I knew it. Perhaps I'd always known it.

I look at Joanna, willing her to continue. I know she's going to wound me, but I want the worst, the whole truth.

'He's got a concert at Manchester tonight, he's filling in for Maguire at the last moment. 'That's why she went off so suddenly. He doesn't mind her turning up on his out-of-town appearances as long as she stays away from London.'

I try to say something but fail. My mouth opens and shuts but no words come out.

'He's a bastard,' Joanna continues, 'She knows that. All the same, I don't think she'll ever get over him.'

We regard each other with sadness. I watch her putting cream on her face, wiping it off with a tissue. I catch her eye in the oval mirror over the dressing-table.

Suddenly I know something else. Joanna knows and has always known about Fanny and me.

'Why do you let it go on?' I ask her as she comes to bed.

'How could I stop it?'

'I don't mean Fanny and Anton, I mean Fanny and me. Why don't you put a stop to that?'

'She needs you,' Joanna says simply. 'She needs you, Paul. And you see, I need her.'

It all clicks into place, smoothly and horribly. Even the reason for Joanna's father being so ready to accept me all those years ago: I was probably the first man she'd ever liked.

Nothing has changed, I tell myself. Fanny will be back. Tomorrow perhaps. Tomorrow evening I'll be able to wander down to see her after supper.

'How was Fanny?' Joanna will ask afterwards.

'Tired. She sent her love. She's coming up to see you tomorrow.'

Nothing has changed, I tell myself, nothing has changed.

'Goodnight love,' I manage to say. 'Sleep, now. Don't worry any more about anything.'

Oh Fanny. Everything has changed.

Luminous and Forlorn

'You can come to my place tonight,' Neville whispers to me before school on Monday. 'My parents are having a night out. What do you say? We can have some wine and some beans on toast and we'll dance after. What do you say?'

'Oh Neville, I don't know. I've got my Milton essay to finish and you know I'm only allowed out on Saturday.'

His eyes hold mine. 'Make some excuse. Say there's something on. Something educational. Come on. We'll have a great time.'

He squeezes my hand before I rush off to my prefect duties.

Neville is incredibly handsome. He looks like a young Cary Grant. Everyone says so. Eyes brown as toffee and the same cleft in the chin.

All the same, I know I won't be able to persuade my mother to let me go out with him on a Monday night.

She's never met Neville, but even so, she's dead set against him, her lips becoming thin as little whips whenever I mention his name.

His family is English, which is bad enough, and they keep a licensed restaurant, which is worse. 'Pubs are one thing,' my mother says. 'Pubs are the known enemy. But when cafés, which have always been decent places where decent people can go, start to offer alcoholic drinks, well, it's the thin end of the wedge and a trap to the unwary.'

The way my mother brings out 'alcoholic drinks' you know it's no use trying to break it to her that Neville is your boyfriend.

She doesn't object to you having 'friends of the opposite sex,' but she won't have anything serious that might put you off your studies, mind. And in any case, she wouldn't have Neville.

What she'd really like is if I still went out to the pictures with Nia Gruffydd every Saturday night, because Nia Gruffydd is one of these girls who wears pleated skirts and hair bands and no trace of make-up. Oh, she's nice enough, but I often wonder if she isn't a bit retarded. She's the same age as me, going on seventeen, but she looks fourteen, with a chest instead of a woman's body, and her idea of a good time is to go to hear Côr-y-Castell rehearsing.

Anyway, my mother idolizes her, because her mother writes articles in the *Cymro* and gives talks on the wireless.

'If you pass your exams and go to University, you can become a WEA lecturer like Nia Gruffydd's mother,' she's always saying.

Nia's got a brother called Garmon and I'm sure my mother's secret dream is that he'll fall for me one day. She's always asking after him. He's in his second year at Bangor doing Welsh and Philosophy or something, and of course a safe, long-distance courtship by letter would suit her down to the ground.

'Garmon's going back at the weekend,' Nia tells me in History, which is our first lesson.

It's funny, but she's really fond of her brother, though he's so fat and sweaty. Once I called for her and the sitting-room ponged of feet, which must have been him, because whatever you can say about Nia, her personal habits are exemplary.

'Would you and Garmon like to come to a party tonight?' I ask her.

'A party?'

Her big round eyes seem about to pop out of her head. For a moment I imagine two lumps of blue jelly landing on her History textbook.

'A party,' I say, trying to sound cool. 'At Neville's. His parents are going out. We can have sandwiches and wine. And we can dance.'

'I can only do the quickstep,' Nia says. 'Don't ask me to rock-around-the-clock, will you.'

We both smile. Sometimes I think the girl's got the beginnings of a sense of humour.

Miss Mathias comes in then, and just before I settle down to the Repeal of the Corn Act 1842, I feel a cold shiver at my cunning. I've managed it. Got my way again. My mother would never refuse to let me go to a party with Nia and Garmon Gruffydd.

Neville doesn't seem to mind that I've asked Nia and her brother to join us. 'More the merrier,' he says. 'Brynmor's coming along as well. To play the piano.'

I toss my hair back – it's something I've been practising in the mirror. 'Brynmor's always following us around. He's got a piano at home.'

'I know. But his mother doesn't like him playing dance music.'

Poor dab. Brynmor's mother is worse than mine. Not only chapel three times every Sunday, but prayer-meeting and Band of Hope as well.

All the same, I wish he didn't have to follow us everywhere, it's inhibiting for one thing, and humiliating too.

Neville and I park ourselves in one of the little shelters on the prom for a snog, and bloody Brynmor turns up and stands about in front of us and starts talking about Yeats or Schubert or someone, as though that's what we're there for.

I suppose it's worse for Nev than for me because he doesn't have the slightest interest in poetry or music.

God, I never mind having a natter with Brynmor at the right time and place, but when you're sprawled out over somebody, hoping for some sort of vibrant sensual experience, it's just not on.

'Brynmor, go away, will you?'

And what I really can't take is that it's usually me, not Neville, begging him to take the long walk on the short pier.

When you come to think of it, Neville is pretty half-hearted as a lover. His kisses, for instance, are so long and gentle that I could honestly plan out my homework while they're going on and sometimes do. On and on, never changing gear, never reaching any next step.

He never even tries to stroke my breasts, doesn't even try to locate them.

Perhaps I'm lacking in something. Everyone whistles at me, but when I'm in a clinch with someone, they don't half get apathetic.

Islwyn Ellis, this boy I went out with before Neville, at least he used to get a bit excited when he started fiddling with the buttons of my blouse. Only when he'd managed to get them undone, he always started grunting, and in the dark, I used to imagine he'd turned into a little pig, and used to push him away.

At least Neville is handsome and six foot tall and at least he doesn't grunt.

My mother is one of these people who's always full of jolly little precepts like, 'It's up to a girl to say no.'

My God, chance would be a fine thing.

'How would you feel on your wedding night,' my mother asks me, 'if you'd already given away your greatest treasure?'

My God, no one's ever made any serious bid for my greatest treasure. It'll be really great having to admit that on my wedding night.

Neville rings me every single evening, hangs about me every lunchtime, writes me long, boring letters with terrible spelling when he thinks I'm in a bad mood, but as for his love-making, it's nothing short of pathetic.

Do I really want to go on going out with him? Sometimes his five-minute kisses make me feel I could be doing something else. Like running a mile for instance.

Why do people force you into telling lies? I feel really depressed at having to give my mother all that stuff about Nia and Garmon. 'Garmon is very keen that I go with them. He's going back to college next week.' I can imagine her planning her announcement to Mrs Williams next door. 'Yes, she's engaged, Mrs Williams fach. To Garmon Gruffydd. Yes, Delia Gruffydd's son. Her that's on the wire-less every Sunday night in 'Wedi'r Oedfa'. Yes, her only son. Oh yes, Mrs. Williams, Welsh to the fingertips. No, Baptist actually, but as long as it's chapel, Morris and I don't mind.'

Why do people make it so difficult for other people, when all they want is to be truthful and decent?

I take ages getting ready. It's not that I want to look particularly terrific or anything like that. It's just that everything is suddenly a bit of a drag. I've made some notes for my *Lycidas* essay and I wouldn't really mind staying in and being able to get to grips with it.

I hope to God I'm not going to turn into one of these intellectual types. Someone in a Welsh tapestry two-piece who's into *cyd-adrodd*. Anyway, I don't look like one. Not yet. As a matter of fact I look more like a photographic model tonight, my breasts pulled up high in front of me in my new Loveable bra. I could be in the running for Miss Cambrian Coast next year, only of course my mother wouldn't hear of me going in for it. So common.

'Yes Mam, I'll be back by eleven. Don't worry, will you. Yes, I'll be all right.'

Of course I bloody will. Same as ever.

I dawdle along the prom.

It's the end of September and the town is ours again; the two chip shops and the milk-bar almost empty.

The tide is out and the seaweed smells green and rich. Usually I only like staring out to sea when I've got an ice-cream to lick; the cold sweet taste of ice-cream really goes with the tangy smell of the sea. (I love smelling and eating; all the vulgar pleasures.)

Tonight the sea is calm, its colour almost all drained away. Whitish sky and pale grey sea. But with light in it. Luminous is a brilliant word. I often use it in essays.

I nearly drowned by those rocks when I was about thirteen.

I was allowed to swim from the first of May, and that year, even though the weather turned cold and stormy, I couldn't make myself wait any longer.

No one else was stupid enough to join me.

God, I must have been mad. After only a few seconds I knew I was in danger. The waves were so high that I couldn't keep swimming. The sea kept sucking me up and throwing me down again and after four or five times, I remember the realization seeping through me that there was absolutely nothing for it but to give up.

But the very next wave threw me against those rocks and I was able to scramble to my feet and stand there, gulping and gasping like a fish in a bucket.

Even wading back was difficult. It was as though the sea was having second thoughts about letting me go.

When I got to the beach, there was a man standing there; in a brown tweed overcoat, I remember. 'You bloody fool,' he said. That's all. 'You bloody fool.'

I pulled my towel round me and was sick, almost at his feet. I remember the sand steaming as I covered it up.

I remember my cotton vest scratching like emery paper as I pulled it on.

Even my face was bruised by the pebbles the sea had flung at me.

I told my mother I'd had a fall.

Tonight, there's only the faintest breeze ruffling the luminous water.

'The Bay Restaurant. Licensed to sell alcoholic beverages.' Neville's house is the last on the prom, tall and grey with flashy red paint. A notice in the window. *Closed.*

Even from across the road I can hear Brynmor Roberts playing away. That old one, 'Begin the Beguine'. For a moment I stand listening. It sounds restless and forlorn with the seagulls mewing in the background. Forlorn is another of my favourite words. 'Forlorn, the very word is like a knell.' (I write 'I love John Keats' on all my exercise books.)

Brynmor is a bit of a joke at school because he composes oratorios which we have to sing in Assembly. But he can certainly play Cole Porter. He can play proper music too for that matter, Beethoven and that lot.

He improvises a little fanfare when I go in.

Garmon Gruffydd is sitting at one of the tables with a half-full bottle of red wine in front of him. 'Come to join me,' he says, his voice full and fruity like Mr Isaacs, our minister.

They've got a bit of a dance floor in the middle of the

room, and what do you know, Neville is there cheek-to-cheek with my little pal Nia Gruffydd. And, gosh, Nia is looking almost pretty. She's washed her long straight hair and it's yellow as Madeira cake and she's wearing it in a loose pageboy instead of tied back like a kid. She's got a pale blue angora wool sweater on, and, so help me, she's even got little pointy tits under there.

I'm usually in a tearing fury if any girl as much as glances at Neville, but tonight I feel tolerant, even good-humoured. The thing is, they look really happy together. He seems much more relaxed with her than he does with me and she's gazing up at him as though she's Cinderella and it's two minutes to twelve.

When the music stops, they start walking over towards me but I raise my glass and smile at them and Brynmor launches into something else and they go on dancing and staring at each other.

I take a swig of the wine Garmon's poured out for me. It doesn't seem all it's cracked up to be in poetry; all that wine and roses stuff. In fact it tastes a bit like Gee's Linctus. I suppose it's about as romantic as cocoa if you think of it as alcoholic beverage.

I drink about half a glassful and then Garmon asks me to dance.

I get to my feet, neither eager nor reluctant. Garmon is certainly not the most desirable partner in the world, but what choice have I got?

He dances quite well, but I wish I didn't keep thinking about his podgy little hands on my back. He does some fancy turns and breathes down my neck. How much of the alcoholic beverage has he drunk, I wonder? And his mother the champion of total abstinence. I feel quite sorry for Mrs Gruffydd, her son on the red stuff and her daughter in the arms of Neville Cooper of no fixed religion, whose one ambition in life is to get his O-level Maths so that he can join the Marines.

It becomes clear that I'm going to have to dance with Garmon all evening. Well, it would be unfair to expect Nia to dance with her brother I suppose. Especially when she's looking so many fathoms deep in love with my bloody Neville.

But does ghastly Garmon have to press me so tight? Yes, I know about holding your partner close, but this is suffocation. And when I draw in a deep breath, expanding my chest, the nasty little slug gets the idea I'm being provocative.

'I bet you're hot stuff,' he says, nibbling my ear.

'And I bet you're never going to find out,' I say, breaking away from him and pushing him backwards into a chair.

'I'm going home,' I tell Brynmor.

'I'll get Nev.'

I look over at him and Nia sitting close together drinking glasses of pop. 'No, leave him be. He's happy.'

'I'll come with you then.'

'OK. Neville won't notice.'

We let ourselves out into the silent town. 'I didn't know you were nice as well,' Brynmor says.

Why should I bother to flirt with Brynmor? 'As well as what?' Why should I say it? I know that I'm competently put together and prettily coloured-in too; brown hair, brown freckles, blue eyes, pink nipples.

When we get to the pier, we stand listening to the sea dribbling onto the pebbles. 'Do you know the Sea Symphony?' he asks me, 'By Vaughan Williams?' His head moves in time to some forlorn music.

' "For Lycidas is dead," ' I say, ' "dead ere his prime." ' Tears sting my eyes. I want to live for ever.

'Debussy,' Brynmor says, 'Franz Mahler, César Franck.' He sounds like someone praying.

' "Who would not sing for Lycidas? He knew himself to sing and build the lofty rhyme. He must not float upon his watery bier unwept and . . . something in the parching winds." '

'Welter,' Brynmor says.

'Yes. "He must not float upon his watery bier unwept and welter in the parching winds." '

'I might set that to music,' Brynmor says. 'Cello and a lot of percussion. Milton's Lycidas in E minor.'

'I nearly got drowned once,' I tell him. 'Out by those rocks . . . of course I shouldn't have gone in. It was very stormy.'

A moment's silence. 'Anyone can make a mistake,' he says then. He seems to be forgiving me. For something. We turn towards the town. Terrace Road. Bath Street. Past the chapel where he plays the organ. He tells me I can come to listen to him practising. Any time.

Our shadows go before us. Brynmor used to be a midget, but now he's nearly as tall as I am. Curly-haired and eagle-nosed. 'It was a good party,' he says after a while, 'but I don't think I'm going to come all the way up Penglais with you.'

'That's OK,' I say. 'It's no distance from here.'

For a minute or two we lean against the wall of a house in Maesderw Road and watch the moon come out from behind a cloud and the sky lighten. 'Farewell sweet prince,' I say then, and start to run up the hill. I can still hear sea music in my head, and I'm alive, alive.

A Durable Fyre

Two whole days by the sea, Jane told herself in the taxi. A train journey – they rarely went anywhere by train – coca-cola and an apricot pie at the station buffet if they had time to spare, glossy magazines, paperbacks and chocolates.

Yet all was not well; she knew it.

Her mother, who was usually so excited at any little adventure they shared, was quiet and rather aloof, as though she had far rather be at home.

'We're going to see a friend of mine,' she had told them as they had arrived home from school earlier that day. 'You don't remember him, but he's a very old friend. He and his wife have been living in America for almost ten years; they've come back for a few weeks, and he telephoned asking me to take you down to visit them. They've taken a house at Brighton.'

'Ace,' eleven-year-old Miranda had said. 'I'll have to miss tomorrow's clarinet lesson. Have you packed my yellow sun-dress? Have they got a boat? Will we still be able to ride on Sunday? Have you remembered my badminton racquet?'

'Is it Edward and Katie?' thirteen-year-old Jane had asked. They always had a Christmas card from America, invariably the first to arrive.

'Yes, darling, that's right. Edward and Katie Lucas. You'll like them.'

'Is Daddy coming with us?'

'No, he's got a class tonight and a faculty meeting

tomorrow morning. He'll go to Granny's on Sunday. It'll be a nice change for him.'

Getting ready to go, their mother fussed over them, insisting on their wearing last year's cotton dresses which were frilly and childish instead of their new grey dungarees. Miranda pouted, even Jane thought it a little odd.

Then, at the last moment, her mother changed her own new, wide-shouldered blue linen suit for a plain cream blouse and skirt. She was obviously uneasy; the visit possibly something of an ordeal, Jane thought, like going to a funeral or to someone's sick-bed.

Even on the train, her mother couldn't seem to relax. 'Shall we do this quiz in *Girl*?' Jane asked her. 'It's one of the daft ones you like. "Are you ready for love".'

'Not just now, darling. I've got a bit of a headache. You and Miranda do it, and you can try it on me later.'

Luckily Miranda, deep in a Snoopy book and a bag of crisps, didn't raise her eyes; Jane had no wish to waste time on her sister. She cared only about her mother.

Jane loved her mother so much that it was a burden to her. She was so beautiful, that was one thing. Not just attractive like Millicent Knight's mother, not a sexy weirdo like Francie Lane's, but really beautiful. She had deep brown eyes and curly brown hair, her nose was fine and straight and her lips were soft and kind. Her name was Olivia and it suited her; she was brown and feminine and warm.

She was proud of her, too, because she was a famous actress. Well, perhaps not a famous one, but certainly a very good one. She had worked at the National Theatre and on the West End. She occasionally worked on television too, and in worthwhile plays by famous authors like William Shakespeare and Harold Pinter.

Sometimes, she'd be in the park or in a shop with her mother and she'd notice a woman nudging her husband; see them turning to stare after them. Her mother would pretend not to notice that she was being recognized, but it always made her raise her head a little, made her smile her soft, inward smile.

'You're so beautiful,' Jane would say sometimes, as her mother came in to her bedroom to talk and say good-night.

'Oh darling. I'm getting old. Nearly forty.'

'You're not old. You look like Ava Gardner – that's what Daniel Carey says – and she's supposed to be the most beautiful woman in the world.'

'Daniel Carey,' her mother would say in her tenderest voice. 'You and Daniel Carey are two sillies.'

Daniel Carey was one of her mother's closest friends. He was a very well-known television actor, one of the stars of 'Cross Gates Farm'. When her mother had once sent him to fetch her and Miranda from school, the other girls had been green with envy.

'He's just a friend of my mother's. They were in a play together last year. He's always in our house.'

It was true. Her mother did quite a lot of entertaining, and Daniel was one of the regulars. He would help with the cooking, wearing any silly apron to hand, then pretend to be a butler, answering the doorbell and announcing people like they did at a banquet, and afterwards would insist on taking over the washing up. He was one of the few people her father could be relied upon to recognize. 'Ah, Daniel,' her father would say in his rather hearty, company voice. 'Nice to see you again, Daniel old chap.'

Her father never seemed to mind all the outrageous attentions Daniel paid to her mother, indeed, seemed to encourage the relationship between them. Whenever he was too busy to go to the theatre or to a concert – he was a

Mathematics lecturer in University College, and usually
busy – he used to suggest that Daniel should use his ticket.
'Ask Daniel Whatsisname to take you,' he'd say. 'It'll be
just his cup of tea.'

'Oh, but isn't he handsome,' Jane's best friend, Clare
Cunningham would say, whenever Daniel's name cropped
up. 'You're so lucky. He practically lives in your house. He
seems to be there much more than your father. Do you think
that your mother might . . . you know . . . adultery and so
on?'

'Oh no, there's no question of that,' Jane would answer,
with a great show of conviction. 'Neither of them goes in
for that sort of thing. Neither of them is at all . . . well . . .
lustful.' All the same, she often felt a thrill of danger in the
situation. She loved her father, of course she did, but was
quite aware that he might be considered rather dull.

'He's married to his work,' her mother would tell her
friends. 'He lives – quite contentedly – in a world of
equations and formulae. We'd been to a ballet the other
week, one of those modern ones, and I was complaining
about the second half. "Weren't you bored, Lionel?" I asked
him. "Not in the least. In the second act I managed to work
out a problem which had been bothering me all week."'

'Don't you mind that Daddy always puts his work first?'
Jane would ask her mother sometimes.

'Not at all, darling. We've been married almost sixteen
years. We're not young lovers. He doesn't have to pay court
to me any more, he can be himself. That's why we get on so
well. He has his interest, I have mine.'

But what about love, Jane wanted to ask. Getting on well
is one thing, but what about 'the durable fyre in the mind
ever burning?' She pondered on words like rapture and
ecstasy. Her mother and father were beyond that stage
perhaps. But what if Daniel was still there?

Would it be altogether surprising if her mother decided to leave her father for the younger man, who fell on one knee as he brought her flowers – though they might only be a few tulips he'd picked from their own garden – and who called her his plum blossom and princess and his heart's light, who was always attentive, who could always be relied on to raise her spirits?

Would it be *at all* surprising? For love, whatever it was, didn't seem a great respecter of marriage vows.

Jane sighed. She thought such a great deal about love, had read everything she could lay her hands on, from *Wuthering Heights* to the rude letters at the back of magazines, but still couldn't quite fathom it out; something about it always seeming just beyond her grasp.

It was a beautiful May evening. The train was rushing past fields of buttercups, hedges of blackthorn and cow parsley, rounded hills, copses of trees tipped with green. Yet her mother, usually so alive to the beauties of the countryside that they had to beg her, when driving, to keep her eyes on the road, seemed totally oblivious to it all.

'Tell me about him,' she broke out, suddenly feeling that she had to share her mother's worries. 'This Edward Lucas.'

'What do you want to know about him?' Her mother seemed to be surfacing from a considerable depth. 'He's just a very old friend. You'll like him.'

'Is he an actor?'

'Yes. Well, he seems to spend most of his time directing nowadays, but he still does some acting, I think. He's a good actor, or used to be. He was with the first company I ever worked with: Birmingham Rep. Over twenty years ago.'

'Twenty years ago? When you wore false eyelashes and had your hair cut like a helmet?'

Jane waited. Her mother usually loved to talk about the

Sixties when she wore dresses short as tunics, steel breast-plates for jewellery, and met Mick Jagger at parties. This time, she sighed and said nothing, absolutely nothing.

She tried again. 'Why did he go to America? Was it to make films?'

'Not really. It was because his daughter married an American and went over there to live. His wife – Katie – she's never been very strong, and – well – they only had one child, and naturally she missed her terribly. That was the main reason . . . I think.'

Jane felt, once more, her mother's reluctance to talk about Edward Lucas. Her voice had taken on a harsh note and her hands were restless. Why had she felt that they had to visit him?

'I wish Daniel was with us,' she said.

'Whatever for?' her mother asked.

'He can always make you laugh.'

'But sometimes I don't want to laugh.'

'I don't like it when you're sad.'

Her mother took Jane's hands in hers and kissed them. 'Don't worry about me, darling. I shall be all right. Honestly.'

'Hey, listen! What are two rows of cabbages called?' Miranda, having the first vague intimation that everything was not quite as it should be, felt called upon to exert her-self.

Jane and her mother turned blank faces towards her.

'A dual cabbageway. Listen! What's black and white, has eight legs and signs on on television?'

'I think we've arrived,' Jane said stonily.

On the platform, a middle-aged, almost elderly man hurried towards them. He was tall and thin and grey-haired. Jane's first feeling was one of relief. There was absolutely nothing sinister about this man.

He took their mother's arm, though hardly looking at her. 'Jane and Miranda,' was all he said. His eyes wrinkled up as he smiled. He had a kind, slightly troubled face.

He hadn't seen their mother for nearly ten years, yet seemed almost abrupt in his dealings with her. 'Come,' was all he said. (Jane couldn't help thinking how different he was from Daniel Carey.) And after a moment or two staring at her – Jane – and Miranda in turn, 'Come,' he said again. 'The car's right outside.'

He picked up their weekend bags and led them to his car. 'Shall we have a few minutes by the sea? I told Katie you might feel like a breath of sea air before going up to the house. It's only quiche and salad for supper. Nothing that can't wait.'

Jane sat in the back of the car with Miranda, her mother in the front with Edward Lucas. 'Is it good to be back?' she was asking him in a strained little voice. 'It is,' he said. She saw him nodding his head vigorously.

'Ah, we're in time for ices,' he said then, as they reached the Front.

He turned and handed Miranda a handful of coins. 'What shall I get?' she asked.

'Whatever you like. Spoil yourselves.'

Jane would have preferred to stay in the car with her mother, but she knew that elderly people expected you to be pleased, even excited, about ice-cream, so she smiled her thanks and followed Miranda.

As they stood in the queue at the ice-cream kiosk, her mother and Edward Lucas got out of the car, too, and walked as far as the sea-rail. And turning in their direction, somehow compelled to turn in their direction, Jane recognized something familiar, unfamiliar, rare, terrible, in the way they looked at each other.

Oh, that look. It resurrected a blur of hazy agitations

which had lain buried in her subconscious mind for years; perhaps of the time immediately before Edward Lucas had left for America, of her mother, withdrawn and ugly with grief, of her father who had had to put aside his work to take on a mother's role; of all these things and other dark, floundering half-submerged things. 'Oh, Mama,' her heart cried.

The wind blew, suddenly chill, from the sea. 'Oh, Mama,' her heart cried as she licked her scalding ice-cream.

Romeo's Cousin

A wonderful midsummer evening in 1979. The party was in the house of Charles S. Grosvenor, chiefly known for being rich, but also as a patron of the arts and culture vulture.

We don't have all that much culture in Brinsley, but from time to time a theatre company from Bristol, Birmingham or London drops by for a week during a provincial tour, probably because of the river walks and the famous moors and Mr Grosvenor's lavish Friday night parties. Also we have a new theatre, small but with excellent acoustics, converted from an old warehouse.

In my capacity as assistant town librarian, I make it my duty to set up a table with artistically arranged publicity material, which always catches Mr Grosvenor's eye if no one else's, so that I always get invited to his theatre parties. This time I was on my own, so I didn't bother with the chicken pieces in mayonnaise or the salmon and avocado mousse or the mounds of salads, but homed in on the chilled white wine and later the strawberries and cream and the slightly warm white wine. It was a magical evening, a heady smell of honeysuckle in the garden and of other, mostly white flowers which I didn't recognize, in the conservatory and the vast drawing-rooms, but I wanted to get fairly drunk fairly soon because I was celebrating my divorce and I was no longer a hundred per cent happy about it. Geoffrey and I had had an open, low-key marriage, no great thrill even at the beginning, but he was a nice, friendly bloke and I knew I was going to miss him because he always knew what to do when anything fused or jammed or blew up or simply fell off the wall and also he could always make me laugh, even when I was most angry with him.

I wasn't at all angry when he started to go out with Violet Armitage; she was interesting and fairly nice-looking and was soon fitting in with our crowd. After all, I was seeing other men, so it seemed only fair that Geoffrey should have Violet. But yes, I was certainly put out when he told me he'd fallen in love with her and wanted a divorce, though I couldn't make any great issue of it, because it was a risk I'd taken. We'd both taken that risk. In the Seventies, having a great time with no strings was considered the most important thing in a marriage.

Even on that evening when he should have been out celebrating with Violet, he offered to come with me to the party, but of course I had to say no, that I'd invited Bob Chance ('the devastating Bob Chance', Geoff always called him), and that I'd be quite all right, thank you.

And I suppose I was all right. I had a new black chiffon dress and silver highlights in my hair and the night was warm and moonlit and several men were looking at me, signalling that they were available – for a while at least – and several women were looking in my direction and looking away again very quickly, which is always gratifying.

At about midnight, there was dancing on the terrace and at first I was just drunk enough to enjoy it, but after a while and a couple more drinks, I started feeling light in the head and heavy in the feet and wandered off into the garden and almost at once realized that I was being followed, so I waited.

'Hello,' my follower said. 'I hope you don't mind if I join you out here.'

'Not at all. I was hoping someone would. After a while it gets just too hot for dancing, doesn't it?'

'Indeed it does. You dance very nicely, by the way. I was watching you.'

'I was watching you, too. Watching you watching me.'

'You dance so well.'

'Do I? No I don't. I don't think you know too much about dancing. Geoffrey always says I bounce about too much.'

'But I always think that's a very good fault. In fact, I think women who don't are not adding much to the sum of human pleasure. You were. You seemed bent on it. Full of joy.'

'It's just the way I dance. I can't dance any other way. I'm not really full of joy. Not tonight, anyway. I've just had a divorce and sometimes it doesn't seem a particularly good idea. Are you divorced?'

'I'm not even married.'

'No, you're too young. Listen, weren't you in the play tonight?'

'Yes, I was. Were you there?'

'Rather. In the fifth row of the stalls with the official party. Weren't you Juliet's cousin? Or was it Romeo's cousin? The one who gets stabbed?'

'Well, Romeo's friend. But I did get stabbed, yes.'

'You were very good.'

'Getting stabbed?'

'No, all the way through. No, I thought you were very good. Honestly. I like actors. I met one last year. Philip somebody. P'raps you know him? A few months later I saw him in a play on television. Do you do television?'

'When I'm asked. But I'm not very often asked. Hardly ever, in fact.'

'Never mind. You will be. You're very young, aren't you?'

'That's the second time you've said that. Come on, you're not so old yourself.'

'I'm thirty-two. How old are you?'

'Thirty.'

'No you're not. Maybe twenty-five. I'm a bit drunk, by the way.'

'I won't take advantage of you, I promise.'

'You certainly can if you'd like to, but it's entirely up to you. I don't want you feeling sorry for me or anything like that.'

'No, what I feel seems to be lust rather than pity. How do you feel about good old-fashioned lust?'

'To be absolutely honest, and I'm not often even moderately honest, it doesn't seem to be the old all-in-all, these days. I used to think it was positively the only thing, but now I seem to think other things, things like affection and, well, being comfortable together are quite important too. What do you think?'

'At the moment, I can't think of much beyond this lust business. You're so lovely, that's the trouble. It's all these curves and slopes. Oh, I just love the way you're so round and so flat, so up and down and so on. "Straight leg and quivering thigh." Oh, so lovely, have I said that before? "And the demesnes that there adjacent lie." He knew a thing or two, didn't he, the old boy? So soft and wet and lovely. Perhaps we can wait till afterwards to discuss affection and so forth. What do you say?'

'By all means. But I don't think we're going to be very comfortable here, do you? On these pine needles? Oh well, yes of course. Under the stars. Under the stars.'

He was about twenty-five; very beautiful, very ardent.

He came home with me afterwards and it was bliss to stretch out on a big soft bed. But it was four or five o'clock by this time and though he was making a great effort to tell me how wonderful I was and how wonderful it had been for him and how wonderful it was that we were going to have this wonderful relationship, he could hardly keep his eyes open, so that after a bit I turned him on his side and he went straight to sleep.

The next morning I had to go to work so I left him a note. 'By the way, by name is Anne Daley. Help yourself to bacon and eggs and coffee. A. Daley.' I couldn't think of anything else to say.

I phoned the house at one, but he'd left. (I discovered later that he'd got a matinée.) Of course I could have gone to the theatre that evening to find him, he could have come back to find me, but neither of us made the move; it wasn't fated to be more than a one night stand, though a very sweet and memorable one.

And it became more memorable as time went on because I discovered that I was pregnant.

Of course it was all my fault. Everyone was on the Pill in 1979. How could he have guessed that I'd decided to come off it because of some scare story I'd read in the library about its long-term effects? Why the hell couldn't I have remembered I'd come off it? Pregnant and stupid. Oh bloody hell.

The next few months I spent feeling sick, trapped, furious, deciding on an abortion, deciding against an abortion and then feeling sick, trapped and furious again. I managed to go to work – occasionally a little late – but apart from that I hardly stirred from the house.

Geoffrey and I still saw each other occasionally and he was the first to notice my condition.

'Look, I think we ought to get married again,' he said. 'This thing with Violet isn't working out too well and I'd be quite glad of the excuse to finish it. We'll tell her that we spent the night together to celebrate our divorce and that this happened.'

'As a matter of fact, that was the night it happened.'

'I thought it might have been. I gatecrashed the party to check that you were all right and stayed just long enough to see that you were.'

'He was one of the actors. He played Romeo's cousin. I never found out his name.'

'You would have if he'd been important to you.'

'He wasn't important to me. But nice all the same. Very nice. I don't want you to think it was just anybody.'

'Shall we get married then? Remarried I mean?'

'Are you sure you want to?'

'Quite sure.'

'Does that mean we have another honeymoon?'

'Of course. Where shall we go? Madeira again?'

So Geoff and I got married for the second time. Violet wasn't altogether thrilled about it, but I invited her to be my bridesmaid and luckily she found that quite amusing, particularly since she looked so much prettier than I did. (At that time, I mean, my old white dress two sizes too small.)

And this second time, we seemed to settle down. Little Joe was born after a few weeks and within two years I had Emily Jane and in no time at all Geoffrey and I had become a proper married couple, spending our Saturday afternoons in B&Q looking at motor mowers and our Saturday evenings with a video and a couple of take-aways.

Violet is married to a dentist and has very troublesome twin boys. Geoff always calls her 'my ex' but she doesn't seem at all important to him. I never think of my past men-friends. I saw the devastating Bob Chance the other day and he'd become fat and bald; I hardly recognized him.

Then, two or three months ago, I saw *him*, Romeo's cousin, on television. He was playing a leading part in a play about the Gulf War. He'd filled out and become very handsome and I nearly fainted with pride. Or perhaps it was desire.

'Look,' I told Geoffrey. 'That's him. That's him.'

Geoffrey snatched up the Radio Times. 'He's called Basil Hargraves. Basil. No wonder he didn't tell you his name. Why don't you write to him? Care of the BBC?'

So I did. 'Dear Basil Hargraves. My name is Anne Daley and we met one night in 1979 when you were touring in

Brinsley with *Romeo and Juliet*. I'm so glad you're being asked to do television now. I saw you tonight and you looked very handsome and grand. I wonder if you remember that midsummer party when we met? I was very unhappy that night and you did something for me which put me back on the right track. Thank you for that and the very best of luck.'

I didn't get any reply for a few weeks and then I got a postcard with his photograph on one side and 'With best wishes Basil Hargraves' printed on the other. I threw it straight in the bin, but later I got it out again, wiped it clean and put it in my underwear drawer.

Geoffrey teases me about it.

A Most Moderate Lust

It was a small private ward with pale pink paintwork and pink floral curtains. The bed and the armchair were covered in a deeper pink.

'How pretty,' Laura said. She sat gracefully at the bed-side, letting her coat fall open as she sat. Her coat and dress exactly matched her wheat-coloured hair.

'I loathe pink,' Rosamund said sharply. Though feeling at a disadvantage, she was far from cowed. She was, after all, a very attractive woman. Her white satin nightdress had insets of hand-made lace.

Laura's eyes, having already registered the Reger night-dress, rested on the enormous bunch of bright pink tulips on the glass and chrome table, conspicuously the only flowers in the room. From Philip of course.

'I hope you don't mind my coming. I've been worried about you. Honestly. And Philip's been quite frantic.' The ugly, ill-chosen flowers made her feel particularly generous.

She freed the bunch of hot-house grapes she had brought from its several layers of tissue. It was a large, well-shaped bunch, but not large enough to be ostentatious. Absently she picked a pale, almost milky fruit from the underside of the bunch and handed it to Rosamund who accepted it with neither visible surprise nor thanks.

'He wasn't frantic,' she said, 'not at all. Just a bit fussed.'

Laura's fine eyes narrowed. An apt word. It summed up her husband. A middle-aged, handsome but fussed gentleman, whose hair, moreover, was getting rather thin on top.

Rosamund studied the grape she had placed on the palm of her hand. It was a very pale blue, like the veins of her wrist. 'Don't you hate me then?' she asked gently, a little nervously.

'I did at first,' Laura admitted, 'though not a lot. Especially when I realized he didn't seem to want a divorce.'

There was a short pause. 'But don't you want to get married?' she asked then. 'Don't you need a man of your own? Or is that being old-fashioned?'

'He's very fond of you. And proud of you. Don't under-estimate yourself.'

They smiled at each other for the first time, the splendid bunch of grapes between them.

'I don't think you love him very much,' Laura said. With some deliberation she chose the largest grape from the very top of the bunch and ate it gravely. 'But then,' she said, 'I don't suppose I do either. I mean, not the great all-absorbing love one always hopes for.'

Rosamund sighed, seeming to agree with her. She ate the small sour grape Laura had handed her and grimaced like a child. There was something child-like about her. 'It's partly habit now,' she said. 'Like marriage, I suppose.'

'At least you have your career,' Laura said.

'Yes.'

'When I first met you at that Christmas party, I didn't like you at all. I thought you were . . . well . . . rather brash.' As she spoke, Laura pushed the bunch of grapes towards Rosamund as though to mitigate the sting of her words.

'I was very nervous. Perhaps I was over-compensating. It had only just begun then. Just a week or so I think. And after all, you were his wife.' She plucked off several of the choicest grapes. Her smile was either thanks . . . or apology.

'He didn't like it much when you took that job in Saudi

Arabia a couple of years ago,' Laura said. 'To be honest, I thought it was all going to end then.'

'So did I. I cried a lot, I remember. I think I must love him, you know. I certainly cried a great deal at that time.' Rosamund seemed surprised to remember her tears.

'Oh, endings always bring out the most exaggerated feelings,' Laura said. 'Whenever I've been on the point of leaving him, I feel so emotional and helpless and weak that I always stay. Of course, I love the house very much.'

'It's a beautiful house.'

'I didn't realize he'd taken you there,' Laura said, a shiver of ice in her voice. 'When was that?'

'Sorry. Just once or twice when you were in Greece last summer. I didn't touch anything valuable, I promise you.' Rosamund tried to be frivolous.

'You don't care for antiques, I suppose?'

'What makes you say that?'

'Architects usually like great square white ashtrays and spotlights and stiff flowers bundled into acrylic jars.'

'I loved your house. You have exquisite taste.'

'Thank you.' Laura was mollified. 'I have a shop, you know, but I always keep the best pieces for myself. You have a flat, I think, in Battersea.'

'Yes. No square white ashtrays though. No acrylic jars.'

'Do you have any family? Philip told me about your mother dying last year. I was so sorry.'

An orderly brought in tea on a bright pink plastic tray. A minute or two later, she came in again with an extra cup and saucer.

'I'll pour,' Laura said. 'Have you any family?' she asked again.

'One sister, one brother-in-law, two nieces and a nephew. They live in Australia.'

'What very dark tea. Not so much strong as sinister. Is it

always like this?' Laura placed the cup and saucer carefully within Rosamund's reach. 'How long do you have to stay here?'

'The last stitches come out tomorrow. Another two or three days after that, I think.'

'When the phone rang that night, do you know, I was quite certain it was you. I woke up and just knew.'

'I'm sorry I disturbed you. I hadn't anyone else to ring. Philip's number was the only one that came and I was shivering too much to handle a directory.'

'I went in to wake him and told him who to ring and what to do. Do you know, he'd never even noticed that you were looking ill. I'd noticed it at that reception we all had to go to and told Philip so then. But I suppose he thought I was being spiteful . . . You know.'

'I'm nearly forty,' Rosamund said, quite suddenly.

'What of it? I'm forty-six in August. Though I'd never tell anyone else . . . I thought you were much younger though,' she added.

She remembered the time when Philip had first mentioned the new woman in the office. Five or six years ago. 'Very pretty,' he'd said. 'Not a beauty like you, but certainly very pretty. A bit like that Romney portrait of Emma Hamilton.'

They looked at each other kindly. Rosamund put her cup back on the tray and settled back on her pillows, suddenly very tired. She closed her eyes.

'Come and stay with us when you come out of hospital,' Laura said. 'No, I mean it. You'll really need to be looked after for a while. I have nothing much to do, I only do an hour or two at the shop these days. Say you'll come. Please. It'll be so . . . so convenient.'

They looked at each other and suddenly they both laughed, they laughed out loud and laughed again. They gasped for breath and then started again, laughing till the tea tray rattled on the bed. They both became ugly, their faces distorted. It was the sort of laughter that doesn't often happen after childhood and which brings all the intimacy of childhood back with it.

'Oh stop it, stop it,' Rosamund shrieked at last, violently pushing the bedclothes and the tray away from her. Laura pressed the bell and went on pressing it.

'Whatever's happened?' the nurse asked. Rosamund was very pale and her face was wet with sweat and with the tears that were running down her cheeks.

'I'm afraid I'll have to ask you to leave,' the nurse whispered to Laura, as she took Rosamund's pulse. 'Something seems to have upset her.'

As Laura walked down the corridor, she could hear Rosamund's laughter starting up again.

From the first Philip was both irritated and embarrassed by the situation.

Rosamund was introduced to their friends as Laura's cousin, Laura inventing a whole childhood they had shared, even producing snapshots showing the two of them in sunbonnets. 'She was such a pretty little thing,' she would tell everyone, 'even Cook loved her better than anyone else.'

On Tuesdays and Fridays, the evenings that Philip used to spend with Rosamund, Laura made a point of having to go out somewhere, so giving the lovers a chance to be on their own.

'The position is quite intolerable,' Philip said one evening, as soon as Laura had left them. 'I know she wouldn't be capable of planning this just to spite us, but if she had, she couldn't be succeeding better. We're both on edge. It's quite monstrous.'

'I can't see that. Not at all,' Rosamund said. 'After all, the situation has been more or less like this for nearly five years. Laura and I have often met and been quite civilized to each other. This isn't so very different, is it? Anyway, it's only for a short time, only till I'm well enough to start work again.'

'Oh God, when will that be? I know Anthony's pretty fed-up with having your clients breathing down his neck all this time. When will you be well again? Oh Rosamund, will it ever be as it was before all this happened?'

'I don't know, Philip. Perhaps this is giving us time to take stock. Perhaps we should . . .'

But Philip suddenly advanced upon her, pulling her into his arms. He kissed her more and more ardently. 'I need you, Rosamund. I need you. This simply won't do.'

'We must get married,' he said then, thoroughly roused and at the same time worrying about his rapid heart-beat and jerky breathing, Rosamund's sudden illness having given him the first intimations of mortality. 'This won't do at all,' he repeated, his hand on his heart, 'I must regularize my life. We must get married. There's no other way, no other option.'

At last, Rosamund managed to heave him away. 'You seem to have forgotten about my operation,' she said crossly, 'and furthermore you seem to have forgotten where we are. Sit up, Philip. I'll stay here until the end of this week, then I'll return to my flat. But while I'm here, I'm Laura's cousin, so don't embarrass me with any more of this wild behaviour. And please don't say another word about us getting married because we both know it isn't feasible. Now I'd like a large whisky, please.'

When Laura returned at eleven o'clock, she was surprised to find that Philip had gone out.

She and Rosamund had a nightcap together and talked.

Rosamund spoke of the time she had been unfaithful to
Philip during a holiday in Spain. Laura revealed that she
had men friends; one a retired major who took her for
lovely meals in country clubs, the other a literary gentleman,
the grandson of a famous poet, who took her to lectures
and museums and pubs. Both relationships were platonic.

'They restore my self-confidence, I suppose,' she said.
'Anyway, I seem to need them. Both of them.'

'How sad life is,' Rosamund said. 'We all seem to be
filling gaps. Aren't there any relationships that are complete?
Really complete? I've never found one. What about you?
When you and Philip were first married, what was that
like?'

'Disastrous. For both of us I think. For the first year or
two, he seemed to think I was some sort of faulty engine he
could get going if only he tried hard enough and often
enough. When he finally gave up, things got much better.'

'He's pretty insensitive. When I met him first, he seemed
courteous and considerate. I was sick of men who pounced
and he seemed different. When it was too late, I realized
that he was only more experienced in his timing.'

'He'd become fairly experienced by the time he met you
... oh, I hope you don't mind my saying that.'

'Not at all. I gathered quite soon that I wasn't, by any
means, his first girl-friend.'

'No. And some of them were rather frightful. Poor
Philip. At least I was never ashamed to be associated with
you.'

They smiled at each other again; they had become sad,
even sentimental.

It was after one when Philip came home. He was very
drunk and they both scolded him.

'This is an impossible bloody situation,' he said to
himself when Laura and Rosamund had taken themselves

off to bed. 'They don't make up one real woman between them.'

As he worked savagely at his drawing-board, he thought of the time when he had – naturally enough – imagined Rosamund, small and lively, with curly black hair and round green eyes, to be the complete antithesis of his cool and beautiful wife. 'Neither of them,' he told himself gloomily, 'could satisfy even a most moderate lust.'

Some time later, he marched noisily up to his bedroom, casting neither a thought nor look towards mistress's room nor wife's. The next morning, in spite of a vicious hang-over, he set off to the office almost an hour earlier than usual.

On the last day of her stay, Rosamund seemed more loath than usual to get up. 'What a beautiful house this is,' she said when Laura arrived with her breakfast tray at eleven o'clock. 'I *have* been happy here. It's so warm and silent and luxurious. I don't at all want to leave.'

'Stay,' Laura said, her voice harsh with sudden excitement. 'I certainly don't want you to go. Why shouldn't you stay here with us, live here with us? There's masses of room. What could be nicer and more natural for us all? Please stay. Please. Philip will get used to it. He'll have to get used to it. After all it was he who brought us together, wasn't it? And we need to be together, don't we?'

Rosamund fell back onto the bed and they looked at each other as though for the first time.

Words, like a host of angels, seemed to be hovering in the air above them, but they only looked at each other and let them go.

After a few moments, Rosamund stretched out her hand to Laura, who snatched it up, lacing the fingers into hers.

Outside Paradise

The house was very strange, the vast front room a jumble of books and magazines and shawls; there seemed a great number of shawls, over sofas and chairs, pinned up on the walls and just laid about anywhere. I looked about me with slight unease, knowing that my mother would be itching to tidy up.

Every house I'd been to before was more or less like our house, two small, square rooms with highly polished furniture, some carefully placed ornaments, usually copper or brass, a picture over the mantelpiece, mountains and lakes or woodlands in autumn. The size and exuberance of Genista's house took me by surprise. It seemed like a house in an old-fashioned book where they had maids and a nanny.

'Do you have a nanny?' I asked Genista, nervously wondering where she'd put my coat. I was beginning to feel out of my depth and wasn't sure I wanted to stay to tea.

'Heavens no, do you?'

'Heavens no.'

I loved the way Genista talked. She never said 'everything' but 'every blessèd thing'. She said, 'Oh God', and 'Heavens above', and 'Saints alive', and 'Oh bloomin' heck'.

If I said 'Oh bloomin' heck', I'd be sent to my room. My mother had been a teacher before she'd got married and she insisted that my brother and I spoke properly. We weren't even allowed to say OK. My father was a fitter and turner on the railway. My mother clicked her tongue on the roof of her mouth at some of the things he said, 'Keep your hair on', 'I've got the gut-ache', 'I'm going to the dubs'. 'Oh Alfred,' she'd say, 'not in front of the children.'

'Let's find some grub,' Genista said. 'We won't do very well if we wait for the rest of the ravening hordes.'

She led me into a large kitchen which had a black-leaded range and a dresser and a big scrubbed table. It was a bit like my grandmother's, but much bigger. We had an electric stove, a green and chrome cabinet and a small formica-topped table. My mother was proud of her kitchen, it was labour-saving she said.

Genista opened some tins and shook out some biscuits and some pieces of Swiss roll onto a couple of shiny, dark blue plates. 'Do you like tea or drinking chocolate?' she asked me. 'Or shall I make both? I can easily make both.'

Before I'd replied, a tall, very thin woman fluttered into the room. I knew it wasn't Genista's mother because she'd been to school to see the Headmaster the previous week and we'd all stared at her. She was very pretty with a lovely smile.

'Oh Grace,' the tall woman said. 'Darling, if you're making tea could you possibly bring your father a cup?'

'I'm Genista and I'm only making drinking chocolate. Would a cup of drinking chocolate be OK?'

'I'll ask him.' She sidled out again, thin and silent as a shadow.

'Whoever was that?' I asked. I'd never seen such a thin and cold-looking woman. She was wearing a pale blue tunic which matched the colour of her nose and cheeks.

'Maud Illingsworth. She plays the oboe. She's supposed to be looking after father so why shouldn't she make his bloomin' tea?'

'Does your father play the oboe?'

'No, *she* does. Maud Illingsworth.'

'Where's your mother?'

'Probably working in the garden.'

When I had people to tea, my mother stood over them as she passed round fish-paste sandwiches, egg and cress sandwiches, chocolate biscuits and home-made fruit cake. 'Another cup of tea, dear?' she'd ask, her voice always polite even to Vera Hopwood who played with her food and dropped crumbs on the floor.

Genista had only recently moved to the village so she hadn't had one of my mother's teas.

She put two large yellow mugs on the table and poured rich, frothing hot chocolate into them. 'Right-ho,' she said. 'Tuck in. Sugar?' I'd never before had biscuits and cake without two pieces of brown bread and butter first. I put my elbows on the table and dipped my coconut-cream biscuits into my hot chocolate as Genista was doing. It was gorgeous.

'OK?' she asked.

'Oh yes. OK. Thank you.'

We'd finished the biscuits and were starting on the Swiss roll when Genista's mother came in through the back door. 'Hello Valerie,' she said, taking off her muddy boots and smiling. 'I'm so glad you could come.'

'It's Betty,' Genista said. 'Valerie is Grace's friend.'

'Hello Betty. I'm so glad you could come.'

'Thank you for having me,' I said.

She scrubbed her hands at the sink, then filled the kettle and put it on the range.

'Maud Illingsworth came down wanting tea for father,' Genista said. 'But she couldn't be bothered to make any.'

'Lazy cow,' her mother said. And then she sat down in front of the range yawning for all she was worth. She didn't put her hand before her mouth either, but she looked lovely I thought, happy with herself like a cat. When she'd finished her very thorough yawning, she looked at us as though about to say something, but only smiled instead. I turned back to my lemon Swiss roll. Her eyes were yellow, not lemon-yellow but almost gold like a cat's. She heard someone at the door. 'Ah, here's Grace and Rosamund. Ready for a cup of tea, girls?'

Grace and Rosamund went to the grammar school in Newbridge and came home by bus. They were both tall and blonde with long straight hair and pale blue eyes. They took no notice of me, but I didn't expect them to. They were fifteen and sixteen.

'Say hello to Valerie,' their mother said.

They each lifted their eyes in my direction.

'Maud Illingsworth and father want some tea,' Genista said. 'We're going to watch 'Blue Peter'. Come on, Betty.'

I'd have preferred to stay in the warm kitchen to watch the beautiful girls having tea with their beautiful mother who had gold-brown hair tied back in a large bun, a lovely smile and a man's blue shirt which showed a lot of soft white chest, but I followed Genista into a room she called the den.

I sank into a huge sofa, looking around at this second splendid room: I could watch 'Blue Peter' any old time. Here, there was a warm, spicy smell, wooden floors with rugs, velvet curtains, velvet cushions, and on the walls, big paintings everywhere instead of shawls. I got up to look at them more closely. They were all of dark-haired, foreign-looking women, some of them almost naked, some of them dressed as ballet dancers, Spanish dancers or acrobats. They were painted rather carelessly I thought, the black outlines much too thick, the pale pinks and mauves and blues of the skin and dresses running over the edges, the backgrounds hazy. But though I was scornful of the technique, I had to admit that they were definitely . . . not half bad. I walked round them again. Oh Heavens and Oh God, I said to myself, they're bloomin' beautiful, that's what they are. They were so bloomin' beautiful that tears filled my eyes and rolled down my cheeks. I never usually cried, at home or at school. What was happening to me in this house?

'Whatever's the matter with you?' Genista asked. 'Did you want to watch ITV? You should have said.'

I sniffed, 'I've got the gut-ache,' I said miserably.

'Do you want to go home?'

'No.' I didn't want to go home, ever.

'I like the pictures,' I said when I felt I could speak normally.

'Heavens above, do you really? I'll have to tell Father. Most people hate them. No one buys them. That's why we're so bloomin' poor.'

'Did your father paint them? Is he an artist?'

'Sort of, I suppose. Shall we go into the garden now?'

I followed her out through the french doors, down some steps and into the garden. It was already almost dark.

Genista's family had only been living in Glen Ross for just over a month so I knew her mother couldn't be entirely responsible for the lovely garden, but I felt it suited her, that it was the sort she would have planned. It was the sort of garden you saw in films about gardens; a soft shadowy green everywhere with narrow pathways pushing though the bushes and tall trees which went right round the house so that you hardly noticed it from the road. We had a small square lawn and a vegetable patch in the back.

'My mother's been planting bluebells along here,' Genista said. 'Five hundred bulbs.'

'Will I be able to come and see them?'

'Do you like flowers, then?'

'Yes. Don't you?'

'I suppose so.' Her voice was stern; I think she was beginning to suspect that I was soppy. 'Look, here's the old swing. Shall we have a go? Pretend we're kids?'

I pushed her on the swing, she pushed me and then I pushed her again. Her long straight pale-yellow hair gleamed in the dusk like pale seaweed. We stayed in the garden until it was completely dark and then felt our way back towards the bright lights of the house. There seemed to be a light in every window so that it looked like a house on a Christmas card.

We went in through the front door. I hadn't been that way before; the big square hall had brass-framed mirrors, pots of ferns and two glass lamps, one hanging above the other.

As I was wiping my feet on the doormat and looking round, Genista's eldest sister, Marigold, arrived home. I think she was eighteen. She looked just like the other girls except that she wasn't wearing school uniform but a tight red suit and a black satin blouse and her hair was tied back in a pony-tail.

'Hello girls,' she said. 'Has Bill arrived?'

'Haven't a clue,' Genista said. 'We've been in the garden.'

'That's her new boy-friend,' she added when Marigold had gone into the kitchen. 'Bill Bryden. Not too bad. Better than her usual type.'

'I know Bill Bryden. He lives near us.'

I suddenly felt hot and uneasy. Bill Bryden worked in the gas showroom in town. He was nice enough, small and dark and lively, but far too ordinary to have any sort of foothold in this house. He used to go out with a girl called Hilda Bainbridge, the sort of girl who made my mother sniff.

'He's in the Newbridge football team,' Genista said. 'Last Saturday we all went to the game. He scored a goal and we didn't half yell.'

'Did your mother go?'

'No. Just us four.'

I sighed my relief.

'Do you want to meet my father now?' Genista asked me. 'It's entirely up to you.'

'Oh gosh, yes.' I straightened my school tie and patted my hair down.

'He'll call you "young lady". You mustn't mind that.'

'Oh gosh, no.'

We went back into the room with shawls. There was a fire lit and loud music playing. Genista hurried over to the gramophone and turned down the volume.

Her father was quite old, more like a grandfather really, with a lot of grey hair and a grey beard. 'This is Elizabeth Miles, Father. She lives near the school in a house called 2 Edmund's Close.'

He turned to look at me. 'Have they given you any supper, Elizabeth?' he asked. 'Someone's cooking haddock but I haven't been offered any. Why don't you two cut along and see if you can bring me something on a tray. Anything will do, an egg or a piece of cheese. I won't expect haddock.'

'I'll go. Elizabeth can stay and talk to you. OK?'

I swallowed hard. 'OK.' I looked at the floor, then at him, then at the floor again. 'I like your paintings,' I said at last, 'They're not very neat, but . . . I do like them.'

He smiled, took my hand and raised it to his lips. I felt the dry, rough skin of his mouth and the roughness of his beard. He was an artist, a real artist.

I tried to think of something else to say. 'I'm really called Betty,' I said, 'but Genista feels sorry for me.'

He looked closely at me. 'Why?' he asked.

How could I explain?

'She told me you were a demon at sums and top of the class at composition.'

I felt myself blushing. 'Your paintings are really beautiful,' I said. Again I felt tears pricking my eyes.

Genista brought her father a smallish piece of haddock, some bread and butter and a cup of tea. He said she was a good egg.

We left him then and went back to the kitchen where we had cups of tea and soda scones. At the large table, Rosamund was sewing, Grace was learning French verbs and Genista's mother was just sitting, her elbows on the table and her face in her hands. Marigold and Bill Bryden were washing up, laughing a lot and splashing water at each other.

'Stop it, you two,' Rosamund said. 'My blouse is getting soaked. Why don't you grow up?'

I felt sorry for their father, sitting alone with his music and his haddock.

'Doesn't your father like being in the kitchen with the family?' I asked Genista later when we were upstairs in her bedroom. It was already eight o'clock and my father was coming to fetch me at half past.

'He and mother fall out about Maud Illingsworth,' she said. 'She was his model for years and years and he still likes her to visit. Anyway she'll be going back to London soon, so they'll make it up.'

'Was that Maud Illingsworth in his paintings?' I asked in a rush of surprise.

'Yes. Of course that was centuries ago. Her breasts are like tea plates now, Mother says. But he still likes to draw her, heaven knows why. She plays the oboe you know. Would you like to hear her?'

I wasn't sure I would, but all the same I nodded my head.

We went along to one of the rooms at the back of the house and as soon as Genista tapped on the door, it flew open and Maud Illingsworth practically fell out on us. She was dressed in a sort of long robe; pale pink.

'This is my friend, Elizabeth. She would like to hear you play the oboe.'

'Please come in. I'm afraid it's very cold. There doesn't seem to be any heating up here.' Her face was thin and still blue, but not ugly, not exactly. She looked as though she might be a distant relative of the woman in the paintings.

She fetched her oboe and after blowing into it and complaining that it was suffering from the cold, she started playing some music which was very sad and beautiful. I hadn't expected to like it, but I liked it a lot. It was a bit like a last bird at the end of the day.

Then she started on another piece which was even sadder than the first. It was a bit like winter and the cold, a bit like a woman thinking of the time she was young and happy, a bit like saying good-bye. I could hardly get my breath, that's how sad it was.

After a while Genista's mother came upstairs to listen. She stood by the half-open door and when she saw that I was crying, she cried too, and when the music had come to an end and the room was quiet again, she blew her nose and said, 'Please come down and have some supper, Maud. I've got a nice piece of haddock waiting for you.' There was another silence and then they patted each other on the shoulder and when Maud Illingsworth had put her oboe back into its black case, they went downstairs together.

One other thing happened before my father came for me.

Genista and I were down in the hall waiting for him when suddenly we heard a terrible rumpus upstairs, a lot of shouting and banging of doors and more shouting. 'Saints alive,' Genista said. And then Bill Bryden appeared and stamped down the stairs looking very sorry for himself and Marigold came rushing past him, flinging open the front door. 'Don't ever come back here,' she was shouting. 'I never, ever want to see you again.'

He didn't try to argue with her but just walked out into the pitch-black night.

I've never forgotten how miserable he looked or how black it was outside. Outside paradise.

Delia, Oh Delia

Delia Jarman composed herself for another sleepless night. If she didn't manage to get off before her husband started snoring, she was done for. It's like trying to sleep with a combine harvester, she told herself, as his huge snores gathered to a window-shaking crescendo. A moment's silence, a great deflation like letting air out of an enormous tyre, then the thunderous, bed-clothes-lifting snores again.

'He's like an elephant,' Delia told herself. 'He's like a great snoring whale. He's like the fatling, whatever that was, that lay down with the lion and the calf in Isaiah, Chapter 'leven.'

Over and over again Dr Williams had said her husband was to lose weight, but easier said than done, him with such an appetite for his food. And his drink. 'He can't last the winter,' Dr Williams had told her, 'Mrs Jarman fach, he's carrying five stone excess baggage. Think of the strain on his heart.'

Delia tried to imagine her husband's death. Would it be at night? A night like this one? Would he just stop snoring, stop breathing, growing colder and colder at her side? She'd forgive him a lot if he went peaceful and quiet like that, but she didn't expect it for a minute. Oh, he'd roar and bellow and grizzle and moan and make as much trouble as possible, if she knew him. And she did. Hadn't they been married nearly thirty years?

'You're an old bully, Edward,' she said, her little voice like a butterfly rubbing its wings together. 'Everyone thinks I'm going to be heart-broken when you die and your nephew Leias turns me out, but see if I will. I'll have a bit of peace when you die, Edward, and none too soon either.'

She'd got a bit of money put by that her husband knew nothing about. He'd never been mean, she'd say that for him. Whenever they went to town on market day, he always gave her a few pounds to spend in the shops, and she seldom spent much of it. Well, what was there to buy? Clothes lasted such a terrible long time these days. Crimplene now, made out of oil, somebody told her; it seemed everlasting. Even the nylon overalls she wore in the mornings; only show them the water and they were like new again. She needed so little. She'd tried to buy a corset once; she'd an idea that she'd somehow be more of a woman in a corset. (She remembered the intake of breath, the purposeful wriggle and tug as her nicely-plump mother just managed to fasten the first hook on hers.) Though of course even corsets weren't what they were; they used to be pink and splendid with all those white strings and the laths of imitation whalebone ribbing down the sides. Well, she had tried to buy one. But they hadn't had one small enough for her. 'Why don't you try the Junior Miss Department,' the cardboard-faced assistant in Lancaster House had asked her in such spiteful and insolent tones. She'd never gone to Lancaster House after that; bought her stockings and handkerchiefs and other little things in Woolworths where the girls were much more homely. But she put most of her money away. For afterwards.

'Why did you marry the old devil?' Megan Ellis asked her sometimes. Megan was the only close friend she'd ever had. She'd often come to sit with her on a Saturday night and stay until Edward came back from The Sheaf or The Red Lion; wait, then, till he lurched off to bed.

Why did she marry him? Because he'd asked her, of course, and because she was gone thirty and her parents getting on a bit and anxious about her. He'd been what people called a fine figure of a man; gleaming black hair and a big red face, always laughing. Her poor father had thought she was doing well for herself. 'A nice little farm, Delia,' he'd said. 'Plenty of work for you up there.'

She might be small, just four foot eleven and shoes size three, but no one could work harder. She enjoyed hard work. She even enjoyed scrubbing the stone floors of the kitchen and the best kitchen and the dairy and the endless corridors which would have daunted anyone else. 'A nice piece of Durolay you should have in here, Delia,' Megan used to say. 'Aztec Green, say, or Sahara Gold. It would cheer the old place up and save your back.'

Plenty of time for linoleum when I'm gone from here, Delia would think. She liked stone flags, shining blue in any bit of sunshine. She liked work; she couldn't help it. She liked a big tub of washing. She'd been a good housewife, she prided herself on that, and even Edward had been known to say there was no one like her for rearing the orphan lambs.

Anyway, every girl wanted to get married, and only Edward had asked her.

Unless you counted Tim Brynglas. But he was only a farm servant and you couldn't really expect her father, who had his own business, to agree to that. Poor old Tim. He'd had an accident on a tractor so that his own mother didn't recognize him, and it was she, Delia, who had nursed him, stayed up nights with him when he was getting better and shouting with the pain, changing his bandages and dressings as well as a trained nurse, Dr Parry had said. And his mother, poor old soul, had made her take the pair of lustre jugs on the mantelpiece after, and when he was up and about again, he had asked her to marry him, but with her father, there was no chance. 'You shan't throw yourself away on half a man,' her father had shouted. 'Pity you ever went down there to help.'

But half a man, Delia couldn't help thinking, would have suited her so well. Anyway, it wasn't to be. Even her mother was against it. She still saw Tim Brynglas from time to time, hobbling about; his mother dead years ago, of course. Delia often wondered whether he had anyone to look after him.

'Why did you marry the old bugger?' Megan would ask. 'You know he's got another woman, don't you? Of course he has. Mavis Hopkins from Crown Meadow Villas. Everybody knows it. How can you stay here cooking his dinners and polishing his boots for him to go gallivanting about with that brazen piece? You could leave him, you know that, don't you? Of course you could. And he'd have to provide for you too. The law would be on your side.' (The law indeed. There were some things Megan didn't begin to understand. Where would the law be when Edward found out where she was and told her that her place was at home with him?) 'You could go and live in a nice bed-sitting room in one of those big houses in Carlyle Crescent. You could have a little job washing dishes in the warm. You'd be in your oils, girl. No more of his tantrums. And what do you hope to gain by staying? You know he's leaving everything to his nephew, don't you, his nephew Leias, and that weasel-faced wife of his. Everybody knows that.'

Well, he hadn't got a child of his own, fair play. He would surely have been different if only she had had a child. A farmer wanted a son more than any man. As he was always saying, Cwm Wern had been in the Jarman family for seven generations. Delia was thankful that he had his sister's son to leave it to. He wasn't quite a Jarman, but it was better than nothing.

'They breed like rabbits, these little ones.' She remembered old Twm Price – something the worse for drink – whispering that to Edward at their wedding-breakfast nearly thirty years ago, and him laughing his big laugh and looking at her so full of hope. If only the old man had been right!

Why had he married her? That was surely more difficult to understand. Her father, who had sold him some machinery, had brought him home one night for a bite of supper. 'Ted Jarman,' he'd said to her mother. 'Is there any of the chicken and mushroom pie left?'

'We'll find you something better than cold pie, Mr Jarman,' her mother had said. And she and Delia had left their knitting and gone out to the kitchen to prepare a meal. Her mother loved a bit of company.

'He seems a nice, jolly man, doesn't he?' her mother had said.

Delia had though he looked sly – those small eyes so close together – but she had only smiled as though in agreement.

She had noticed him looking at her throughout the meal, sizing her up, as he had shovelled the ham and chips and salad and pickled onions away into his big red mouth.

'I like a man who enjoys his food,' her mother had said, piling more chips onto his plate.

Delia was thirty then, but she still looked like a child with her black curls and her tiny waist. Edward Jarman was forty.

'I'll have to be getting along,' he'd said, after he'd finished eating.

'Early to bed and early to rise,' her mother had said. 'Come and see us again, Mr Jarman. Don't forget, now.'

'P'raps you'd like to bring your wife and daughter up to Cwm Wern one Sunday afternoon,' he'd said to her father in reply. 'It's a bit rough there, mind, since my mother passed away, but I dare say I could manage to give you a cup of tea.'

'Oh, I'd love to see your farm,' her mother had said, 'oh, I'd love it. And so would Delia. Delia loves farms; she's never so happy as when we go to Tregaron to her grand-mother's.'

Delia had felt like a fly in a web. She could have struggled, but somehow hadn't done so.

I wonder if he thought we were rich, she asked herself. My father had a motor car and a van, but in the end he went bankrupt, poor old soul. Perhaps it was only that I was so different from all the women in his family; his Auntie Lil now, she must have been getting on for sixteen stone; every time she went to chapel she got stuck in a pew, the nasty boys from Hendre reciting, 'And I will dwell in the house of the Lord for ever,' as they went past her. Perhaps he just thought I'd be cheaper to feed than a big woman.

Whatever it was, the sly, sidelong glances, full of hope, like a dog eyeing a roast, had soon changed. For years now he had looked at her like the same dog gazing at an empty plate.

'You'll end up in the Geriatric,' Megan was always telling her. 'If you don't go to law, that's where you'll end up, and don't say I didn't warn you.'

Everyone spoke disparagingly or fearfully of Saint David's Rest Home; it might have been the old workhouse. But it held no terror for Delia.

It was three or four years now since she'd first gone to visit old Betty Pandy there. And she'd gone every Friday after that, when Edward thought she was gadding about the shops. Even after Betty was dead she went on going because of the other old dears there who'd got used to seeing her. She'd take them some little gifts; pikelets or fairy cakes or a few fresh eggs, and she'd stop and talk for a while, especially if there was someone feeling low and out-of-sorts and perhaps crying a bit; an old woman crying moved her heart more than a child crying, somehow. And afterwards she'd make herself useful, cutting bread and butter for their tea or just emptying bedpans; anything to help the nurses, who always had too much to do. Week by week she found fresh tasks, and no one objected; they hardly seemed to notice her there.

She thought it was a very nice place. There was a day room with a big colour television, and a pile of magazines. And sometimes there'd be visits from the physios who tried to get some of them interested in weaving raffia mats or making baskets or painting little pictures; it was a bit like being in the infants school again.

Anyway, one Friday afternoon, after a lot of rehearsal in the kitchen at home, she'd plucked up enough courage to speak to one of the sisters about her chances of being taken on as a helper there. 'I'm nearly sixty,' she'd said, 'but I'm still very active. I'm used to hard work; I could keep all the corridors polished, and the wards. Dr Williams would speak for me I'm sure. He says my blood pressure is remarkable for a woman of my age. I've never had a day's illness in my life.'

'But you've got a home, Mrs Jarman, haven't you dear? A lovely farm up on the Foel?'

'Only until my husband dies, Sister, and Dr Williams says he could go any day. He's got a heart you see, and he won't give up the drink.'

'Well, Mrs Jarman, we could certainly do with you here, if the worst comes to the worst. Good domestics are precious as rubies, and we could give you a nice little room in the attic.'

Sister Brown had taken her upstairs there and then, to show her a neat, cell-like room on the top floor. 'It's small, but there you are, you're not very big yourself are you, and it's nice and quiet up here.' Mrs Jarman had looked about her with gentle pleasure; a small chest of drawers, a curtained alcove for a wardrobe, a narrow bed. She pictured her few belongings placed carefully here and there.

'And when I get too old to work,' she said hesitantly, 'I could move downstairs perhaps?'

'Who'd have a better right?' Sister Brown said. She didn't actually know much about the rules and regulations, but if she had anything to do with it, Mrs Jarman should have whatever she wanted; after all, she wasn't asking for much. 'You may have to contribute a little something towards your keep,' she said.

'I've got a bit of money saved. All my own.'

'I'll go and have a word with Matron, then. Matron knows what a good little worker you are. And the ladies in Glyndwr Ward think the world of you.'

'You ought to go to law,' Megan was always telling her, but it wasn't necessary. Leias should have the farm and welcome. She would take her mother's pictures and her own lustre jugs and move out straight after the funeral. She'd take nothing of Edward's.

For a moment she thought of him with something approaching affection. He can't help being rough and nasty, she said to herself. I'll look after him when his time comes; no one will have better 'tendance.

Dawn was breaking when the great snoring stopped and Delia fell asleep.

Not Singing Exactly

I was brought up quite strict, to know right from wrong, to be careful of what you were at and it's stayed with me up to a point. Not that there was all that love involved in it, it was more fear really. Three girls and one boy and my dad left home when I was five and then we had a stepfather before I was seven. My stepfather was the strict one, well perhaps he had to be with four kids around and not his own. My mum had a good job, supervisor in a dress factory and he was some sort of traveller, so there was a fair bit of money, I suppose, and that means you can afford to be decent, paying your bills and so on. My two sisters were older than me and when they left school they got a job together in the Majestic up town and lived in, so there was only my brother and me left at home, he was the youngest of the family, my brother Terry, three years younger than me.

When I was fifteen and longing to be shot of school, I used to skive off home for the afternoon sometimes and just sit around having cups of tea on the new settee with the telly on and the gas fire and dreaming about being married to a really rich man and not have to work for a living, no factory, no shop, not even part-time up the market. One day my mum came home and I told her I'd got a headache and she said she had a headache too, and we sat together drinking tea and she offered me a fag and I said no because of cancer and she said how I was the most sensible of all her kids and she had this fit of crying. And then she told me she hadn't got a headache only she had just had an abortion, but I wasn't to tell Dave – that was my stepfather – or he'd kill her because he was always on about having a kiddie of his own. She cried for about an hour and I didn't know what to do except make her more and more cups of tea. I hadn't realized before that she was frightened of him too, Dave I mean. He could be a devil. I don't think he ever beat her up, not as far as I know, but he used to lay into my brother for any little thing, coming in late, spilling his food, losing his anorak, anything, and it used to turn her stomach, she'd cry and pull at his arm and beg him to stop, please, but he wouldn't. We all hated him, her as well. I only realized it that day.

Anyway that was the day I knew I had to leave home and it was that night I started seeing this boy Rob. Well, I'd had a bit of a chat and a laugh with him before, but that night I went up the park with him, which was the first time for me, and in about six months I got married to him.

It was three weeks after my sixteenth birthday, the wedding, a really lovely summer day. There were two bunches of white roses in the register office so it seemed a bit like a church, a nicer place altogether than I'd expected, quite posh really. My mum and one of my sisters came and my mum treated us to a meal in the Gatehouse after, chicken salad and jacket potatoes and white wine. She'd never even tried to persuade me not to get married, she knew I was pregnant and that there was no way I could live with her and my step-dad after, him being so strict.

'It's a pity you're starting on a family so young,' she said, 'but there you are, you're more sensible than I was and perhaps you'll be careful after this one.' 'For God's sake go to the Women's Clinic in Broad Street,' my sister Rose said, 'they look after you there. If only you'd said something to me two or three months ago you could have got rid of this one.' 'I didn't want to,' I said, because you have to say that, not liking to admit how frightened and stupid you were.

'Well, it's nice they've got a bit of a flat and they can be together and we'll be able to help them a bit, won't we,' my mum said, and I could see how she was pressing Rose's leg under the table and then Rose said yes they'd do their best and gave me a fiver and a fiver from Tina my other sister who hadn't been able to come because she was on lunches.

Rob and me went to Priory Gardens after and I cried a bit because of leaving home which was a nice place except for Dave and because the bit of a flat we had was really only one room, a long damp room without even a lampshade or a proper cooker, with the bathroom two floors up.

'Tell you what, girl, let's grab a hitch to the country,' Rob said. He's that sort of a person, ever so rough, like all his family, but really nice when you need it most. I could never understand why he wanted to marry me, he was twenty-three and there was some really attractive girls I'd see him hanging around with and I was small and mousey with no figure to speak of, though I've got a bit more now.

Anyway it really cheered me up, the thought of going to the country on such a beautiful day. When Dave – my step-father – first came to live with us, he used to take us out every Sunday afternoon for picnics or for ice-creams, usually to the country somewhere, once to Stratford-upon-Avon which was only an hour away but seemed like another world. He used to make a fuss of Terry in those days, he was quite his favourite in those days.

We walked to the roundabout at Highcross and then got a hitch almost at once from a lorry driver and when Rob said we were going on a one-day honeymoon he said he knew just the place and he took us off the motorway to this village and dropped us where there was a sign saying to the river and that's where we went. And we lay down by the side of this wide, slow-moving river and looking up we could see patterns of leaves against a blue, blue sky and there wasn't any cows or mosquitoes or even people. It was like paradise really, and I kept dozing off because of the wine I'd had and I could feel the baby lurching about a bit in my stomach but it was a lovely feeling that day.

We stopped there till about six or seven and then we walked to the pub and we had some beer and crisps and Rob said did they do bed-and-breakfast and the barman said yes and we stayed there the night. I'd never stayed anywhere before except two weekends in Brownie camp, so of course I often think of that country pub, the little clean bedroom with pink wallpaper and the lovely crisp sheets on the bed, but most of all I remember the afternoon lying by that quiet river.

The room we had wasn't too bad at first. I had a job cleaning a couple of floors of this office block which was quite easy except for leaving a nice warm bed at six every morning. Rob used to say he was in furniture restoration, stripping chairs and that which they bought at auction and tried to sell to shops after, but I always knew that whenever he had a thick wad of dosh it hadn't come from that. It used to frighten me because as I said I wasn't used to that sort of a life and I was always nervous of the police coming. Of course I didn't tell my mum.

To tell you the truth I didn't see my mum very often now. Dave didn't want me calling on them. Even though I was married he was always saying I was a tart and that I'd let them down. 'It was all your mother's fault,' he used to say, 'she'd never let me give you a good hiding.' He gave us plenty of good hidings when we were small, he'd once taken the strap to Rose when she was fourteen, pulled her knickers down and laid her over the bed, but my mum had screamed at him that she'd take us all away if he as much as touched any of us again and though he'd pretended to laugh, oh big threat, he never did except for poor Terry. And also I wasn't very keen on my mum coming to see me because of the room being so crowded and untidy specially after Mandy was born. And then I got pregnant again almost immediately and we thought it would be nice to have two close together and after that I'd go to the clinic and ask them to put me on the Pill, but the next one turned out to be twins, two more girls, Tricia and Debbie, so I had three in just over fifteen months and before the end of the year, Rob was in prison for theft, stealing cars and breaking and entering, two years, and there was I, just eighteen and trapped for ever in this long damp room, my only glimmer of hope that Dave would drop down dead with a heart attack so that I could move back home. He's fifty if he's a day and he's always on about the hard life he had in the army and the stress of his present job, so why can't he drop down dead like other men seem to, but no, I never get any luck.

So of course I have to live by shoplifting because my giro doesn't stretch even to the bare necessities and I've learnt that it's no use asking for the things you need because they only send you from one office to another at the opposite end of town, very easy with twins in the pushchair and the other not able to walk more than a few yards so that a simple bus journey is a nightmare and by the time you get there the office is closed or they give you all these forms to fill up and tell you to come back next week. They won't even give you an electric kettle when yours is broke. 'You don't have to use Pampers,' this woman said to me once. I'd like to see her washing nappies for three babies with no hot water on tap and nowhere to dry them, I really would. There's not even enough to buy food with, let alone the

train fare to see Rob once a month. I don't smoke and I
never go out in the evenings but I do get a bottle of sherry
once a week, the cheapest they have, and a paper to see
what's on the telly and nobody can live on less.

I'm not so nervous as I used to be. I've thought about it
and I know it's the only way I can live and that makes it
easier. I hardly ever take anything from the supermarkets
because they've got all these cameras and security, but the
little shops, I tell myself, wouldn't be so likely to take me to
court because they're all doing badly and I reckon it could
make them a bit more sympathetic, though I could be
wrong. There's a small bread shop up our way and it has
one middle-aged woman serving and another clearing up
and I always get my bread there round about half nine in
the morning when it's empty, and when it's being sliced I
nearly always manage to take a packet of sandwiches, egg
or cheese, from the top of the counter and slip it into this
bag I have on the back of the pushchair. You have to be
careful of mirrors, but so far it's always been all right in
that shop. Greengrocers are quite easy, you can almost
always pick something up from the display by the door or
outside, you can usually pick up a cauliflower though it's
not a vegetable that any of us likes, a couple of bananas are
much more useful, mashed banana is a good tea for the little
ones.

It's ever so easy to pick up clothes from a charity shop
because the women who serve there are only there for a
natter and couldn't care less. It's not very nice to steal from
charity, but I can't afford to be choosy and I think the
people who give the stuff wouldn't mind our having it and
I never take more than I need and it's usually only babygros
and little sweaters. Rose and Tina, my two sisters, give me
plenty of cast-offs, though they're not my style, being tight
and rather tarty, but they certainly make Rob's day when I

visit him. I'm fatter than I was and he likes it. Myself, I like something a bit more plain.

Anyway, I had to have some winter boots. Autumn had been a trial, months of pouring rain, and I only had plimsolls. My feet are long and very narrow and nothing Rose and Tina gives me is any good and I looked in all the charity shops as well, so I knew I had to go to the DSS again to beg and fill in forms and go from one place to another like I said before. Luckily, Terry my young brother has just left school and he said he'd come over to look after the kids for me this one afternoon so that I could go by myself without the hassle of getting the push-chair on the bus and so on. The twins sleep most of the afternoon and Terry is quite good with Mandy, tosses her up in the air and turns the music on really loud to make her laugh. He wants to come to live with us, but I'm sure he'd only regret it with no space and washing everywhere. Kill Dave instead, I tell him, but of course, only in fun.

Well, I was walking past some of those smart shops in Cavendish Road to get to the 66 bus stop when a woman comes out of one of the antique shops and nearly knocks me over. 'Excuse *me*,' she says, but the way she says it you know that what she means is, get out of my way you shabby lower-class person, and I've never got the quickness of mind to answer back. One thing about Rob is he's never, ever lost for words. Anyone who's even half rude to him gets it back with knobs on. But me, I only burn inside. That woman makes me feel a hundred times worse than I already was. She's got one of these huge wrap-over coats on, made of so much lovely material, cashmere or something, that would keep a whole family warm and the most gorgeous soft leather boots that you'd never feel the cold again in and I feel a rush of hatred for her and all her sort. The strange thing is that when she disappears from sight, I march straight into the shop she's just come out of – not the sort of place I'd ever go into in a normal frame of mind – quite determined to nick something from there. To get even with her, I suppose, though I admit it doesn't make any sense.

'May I help you?' a saleswoman says. She has silver hair and pointy tits and a face which looks too smooth to be real.

'I'm looking for a present,' I hear myself saying, 'a birthday present for my mother. Something a bit unusual but not too expensive.'

She comes out from behind the counter. I'm surprised that she seems to be taking me seriously. 'What sort of price did you have in mind?' she asks me in quite a pleasant way, not the sort of half-choked voice I'd expected. 'We haven't much under twenty pounds but what we have is very good quality and of course quite exclusive.'

'I was hoping for something about fifteen pounds,' I say, 'perhaps a little brooch in the shape of a fan.' Fifteen pounds, that's a laugh, I couldn't manage fifteen pence on top of the bus fares.

She's getting quite anxious to find something for me, but everything is in cases and glass cupboards so I can't see anything I can lift, though I keep looking around. I must look as restless as a bird in a cage.

'This is pretty and only twelve pounds fifty,' she says and brings out a brooch, a little poodle with a shiny collar. I laugh a bit hysterically because it's such a daft-looking thing. 'Oh it's nice,' I tell her, 'but I don't think it would suit my mother.'

'I see.' She walks off to another stand without closing the case she got the poodle out of and I grab the first thing I can, which is a silver bracelet, and shove it in my pocket. 'I think perhaps I'll leave it for today,' I tell her and walk quite slow to the door, but before I get to it there's a man standing there. I hadn't even seen him at the other side of the shop, but he's seen me all right.

'Could you follow me to the office please,' he says. I make a grab for the brass door handle, but the door doesn't budge. 'Could you follow me to the office please,' he says again in a very gentle sad voice and the woman with silver hair is also looking sad and I don't know what to do but follow him, so I do.

And we get there in spite of my legs feeling like tree trunks instead of legs and he shuts the door and locks it. 'I'm afraid I shall have to phone the police,' he says in the same voice. 'Would you like to put the bracelet on my desk?' It doesn't seem worth telling him about the three kids and Rob in prison and not having boots. I think about it but I decide not to, if I'd been caught with a loaf or a tin of mince it would be different. I don't say anything, just take the bracelet out of my pocket and put it on the desk like he said. We both look at it.

Then I look at him. He's between middle-aged and quite old, the sort of man who looks exactly like any other man in a dark suit, short faded hair and a face like a kid's drawing of a man, straight nose and a line for a mouth. He's looking at me quite blankly without any anger, just blankly. Looking and looking.

'Pull up your skirt,' he says then, his voice shaking a bit.

I take it that he's making a deal with me and I don't even think of refusing it.

I ease it up as far as it will go. It's a very tight skirt I got from Rose, the sort of thin black material that gets very creased. I have these white cotton knickers on, the sort you wear to go to the clinic. He looks at me for a long time and I look at a spot on the wall just beyond his head. I wonder if this if what he had in mind all along.

'Turn round,' he says after what might have been two or

three minutes but feels like thirty. I turn round. I wonder if the woman with silver hair is his wife.

'Can I go now?' I ask after an even longer time.

'Yes. Go now.' His voice is even more shaky.

I tug my skirt down, trying to press out the creases. He's not looking at me. He unlocks the door, opens it and then stands to one side to let me pass.

As I go I pick up the bracelet again and put it on my arm. I didn't think he'd stop me and he doesn't.

The woman at the counter is busy with something and doesn't raise her head as I pass her.

This time the door opens as soon as I pull it.

All the way down Cavendish Road and Market Street I think about the afternoon when Rob and me got married, sitting high up in the cab with the lorry driver, Rob with his arm around me, blowing smoke in my hair and saying rude things to make me laugh. And about lying on the grass by the river, watching the pattern of leaves against the sky and listening to some birds, not singing exactly but making little happy noises.

Then I start to think about where I can sell the bracelet and whether I'll get enough for a pair of boots.

Free

On the first day of her holiday, Ann Richards cycled seven miles to the sea, and though she was a little out of condition after months of studying, she was still full of energy when she arrived.

She laid her bike in the gorse bushes at the foot of the cliff, filled her lungs with the salt air and then ran along the beach, swinging her trainers by their laces, whistling, making a fool of herself and not caring. The future stretched before her, limitless as the hazy horizon.

She was free. University was behind her, sifting through adverts looking for a job still a comfortable way off. Her parents were pleased with her. Six months ago, they'd thought she was going to go under. In the Christmas holidays, she'd had nightmares and cried herself to sleep every night. Her weight had plummeted to seven stone. By this time, she was herself again. She'd got over Jake Holloway. Fought hard and won. She'd known from the beginning what sort of man he was: from the moment she'd first caught sight of him. All the same, she thought she was safe from him, because she was an eager country girl with round face and round eyes, and he seemed interested only in the lean, sophisticated types with blank faces and mud-coloured clothes.

Yet he often seemed to turn up where she happened to be. He called her Blodwen and teased her about the farm at home, though in fact her father worked in insurance. 'Are you coming out with me tonight, Blodwen, or shall you be too busy, look you, with the milking and the mucking-out?'

Why did he bother with her? She was not even beautiful. No one seeing them together would consider them well matched. 'Whatever does Jake Holloway see in that girl?' they'd say. 'She's so ordinary, with her neat clothes and her tidy hair. She's entirely negative. A pretty little thing, nothing more.'

Her room-mate, Sarah Judd, had been quite brutal. 'Jake Holloway goes out with a woman for a month if she will, a week if she won't. Is that what you want? I thought you were after a long-lasting relationship with someone you could trust and admire. I thought you despised the college Don Juans.'

Of course her friend was right. When Jake asked her to go with him to the Christmas ball, she told him, rather primly, that she had other arrangements for that night. 'No you haven't, Blodwen,' he said. 'You want to come with me. What's holding you back?' His eyes were colourless, neither kind nor cruel, beautiful as water. He was a very beautiful young man.

She had broken away from him, but he'd followed her. 'Darling,' he'd said, 'don't look so frightened. Hasn't anyone tried to seduce you before?' And he'd leaned forward and kissed her. She supposed something had happened to her heart. What she remembered was the dryness in her throat and a rush of pain travelling down her body so that she'd almost cried out. The 'darling' – though she realized it meant nothing – had quite broken her resistance; she'd felt it crumble like a stale biscuit. She hadn't tried to evade him after that.

'You want to, don't you,' he'd said a few days afterwards, and she did. And she had; they had.

'It's a good word for it, intimacy,' she'd told her room-mate, Sarah Judd, in a dreamy voice.

'Intimate-off,' that girl had answered.

It wouldn't last, of course it wouldn't. Jake had another thirty or forty years of serious philandering in front of him. There'd be no fairy-tale ending. Ann knew that with an absolute certainty that seemed at odds with her trusting nature. Even her room-mate couldn't accuse her of complacency. 'Are you seeing him again?' Sarah would demand. Ann would never say more than, 'Perhaps.' She didn't begin to count on him.

'Llanelli are playing London Welsh on Saturday. You're not going to miss that, surely,' her room-mate would say. 'Try to hang on to *some* other interests, for God's sake. Why don't we go to Oxford Street this afternoon? See a film afterwards? The whole of London hasn't ground to a standstill, you know. The galleries haven't shut down. There's still art and music and beer. Even a few decent men, if you're prepared to look out for them.'

'Oh shut up,' Ann would say. 'Just tell me whether you're going to be in or out tonight and shut up.'

She had to be ready and available in case he happened to call. She could no longer concentrate on her work. She'd had C minus for her last couple of essays. She realized what she was doing to herself. She'd be like a snail without a shell when he left her.

To everyone's surprise, though, and against all the odds, Jake Holloway's interest in Ann had continued throughout that college year. During the long vac, he'd worked his way across America, but he'd written to her and phoned, and had eventually returned three weeks early, because according to him, he'd suddenly wanted her so much. 'Have you been faithful to me, Blodwen?' he'd asked her, hurting her in his ardour. Of course she had. She wouldn't have dared ask him the same question.

After a week of flawless happiness, the blow had fallen.

He'd told her that he'd been accepted for a year's study at the University of Oregon: he was leaving her.

'But only until next June, sweetheart,' he'd said, pressing his body against hers and licking away her tears as they fell.

Throughout that autumn in Oregon, he seemed to have forgotten her. October and November were terrible months of waiting for the post, months when the phone's ringing pierced her mind, when her heart was so numb and heavy that she felt she could rip it out of her body and feel none the worse.

Then at the beginning of December he'd written to her. About Frankie.

He was shacking up, he'd said, with this great kid called Frankie. He didn't know how long it would last. She wasn't to worry. Frankie was a terrific experience, being with her was like being out in a thunderstorm, but she was to remember that he was still her friend, and he hoped she was having a good year. He very sincerely wanted her to Be Happy. He underlined that.

'She sounds fun,' Ann said limply to Sarah Judd.

'She sounds like a pain in the bum,' Sarah said. 'Do you mind if I open the window? There's a smell in this room and it's coming from the direction of that letter. Shall I burn it?'

Nothing Sarah could say or do helped Ann for those last weeks of the Christmas term. She couldn't eat. She shivered over her books and wouldn't go to lectures.

When she went home for Christmas, her father didn't recognize her, left her standing on the platform while he went out to phone her mother with the news that she hadn't arrived. When Ann, at last, wandered out of the station and found him, he was almost afraid to take her home. 'What the devil's the matter with you? You look just like my poor Auntie Minnie when they took her away to the sanatorium in Brecon.' 'I'm all right, Dad, honestly. I'm tired, that's all. I've been working too hard. I'll be all right after a few days at home.'

Her mother had been equally direct. 'You've had one of these abortions, haven't you?' she'd asked, when she'd got Ann safely in bed and was unpacking for her.

'No I haven't, Mam. Honestly. It's nothing like that.'

She'd cried rather noisily then, and told her mother about Jake and his girlfriend in America. And her mother had said it was all for the best, she'd never liked that Jake, there was nothing homely about him, nothing nice, nothing comfortable. He wasn't right for her in any way. The next day they'd go to Swansea and buy her a lovely new dress. 'Where's the man can ease the heart like a satin gown,' her mother had quoted, while making a mental list of all the eligible young men likely to be at home for Christmas.

'Drop in on the Lloyds before you go to work tomorrow, Dilwyn,' her mother had told her father in bed that night. 'And ask them over for a meal tomorrow night. We haven't seen the Lloyds since the Harvest Supper.'

'Gareth isn't due back from Cambridge till Friday,' he'd replied.

'Drop in on the Lloyds before you go to work tomorrow and ask them over for a meal on Friday night, I haven't seen poor Hester since her operation . . . Oh, Dilwyn, another sweetheart is the only remedy. And by the way, I'm taking her to Swansea tomorrow to buy her that new dress you wanted to get her for Christmas.'

'I thought I wanted to give her driving lessons for Christmas,' her husband had said mildly, 'but I suppose you know best.'

'She used to be fond of Martin Williams. Call in on Megan Fred as you go past; see if you can find out where he is.

She's auntie to Martin's father. I wish I could remember what I read in the *Teify Journal* about Huw George. Was he engaged, say? Or was it just drunken driving?'

Ann had caused her parents much anxiety through the Christmas holiday, though her mother had the satisfaction of seeing her go out three or four times with some of her former boyfriends.

And in the spring term, Sarah Judd had carried on the vigorous programme of rehabilitation. Ann was a popular girl and since she showed no interest in men, they naturally thronged round her.

'Yes, Paul's very nice,' she'd agree with Sarah readily enough. 'Yes, he has a good mind. Yes, fairly attractive. No, I don't want to go out with him again.'

Sarah watched her progress with a sharp eye, chalking up the hours she'd been absorbed in a book, the number of times she'd laughed during a film, the degree of interest she'd shown in the political discussion they'd had with the couple across the passage, the way she'd winked at the bus driver on the way to college and hadn't tried to avoid Jeff and Geoffrey after Anglo-Saxon.

One week in March, after Ann had put on another pound and a half in weight and got a B plus for an essay on Beaumont and Fletcher, Sarah had risked asking her how she now felt about Jake Holloway.

'I have the odd five minutes when I think I may get over him,' Ann had said gravely.

It wasn't quite the answer Sarah Judd had been hoping for.

'Whatever she chooses to say,' she told herself briskly, 'she's improving every day. She's eating more, drinking less, and she's working.'

During the Easter holiday, Ann had gone to Cumberland to stay with Sarah and to her surprise had managed to enjoy herself. When she got back, she was well enough to start studying really hard for her finals.

On her birthday in May, she got a card from Jake which she just stuck up on on the pinboard with all the others.

She was calm and well for her examinations in June.

On the morning of the last exam, she received a short letter from Jake. 'Put away your hot-water bottle and your knitting, I'm coming home. America is out of my system, out of my heart. My heart is full of Blodwen. Stay in London till I come.' She didn't bother to show the letter to Sarah. It meant too little. She pushed it into a litter bin on her way to the Underground and didn't let herself think about it; had no real wish to think about it. She concentrated all her attention on her last paper. And the next day she travelled home.

Her parents were proud of her, proud of her courage. Indeed, she was proud of herself, and the perfect mid-summer day, golden and cloudless, seemed her just reward; she was determined to make the most of it. She swam and sunbathed, ate her sandwiches, played French cricket and raced across the sands with a group of children, collected white pebbles, ate ice-cream and fish and chips and then sunbathed and swam again.

At about six, though the sun was still hot, the beach started to empty, and by half-past was almost deserted. Ann, wanting to prolong the day's mindless pleasures, ran across to join the only child still left, a small girl, two or three years old. 'Shall we build another castle?' she asked her.

For almost half an hour they worked together, saying little, but both quite contented.

When the child's father appeared from somewhere further up the beach, the castle was finished, small to match the small girl, but competently built with turrets and a moat.

'That's a jolly good castle,' he said, crouching down with

them. He smiled and nodded at Ann as though to thank
her.

'Are you coming for your tea now, Gina?' he asked his
daughter.

'No,' she said, without raising her eyes from the castle
which she was still patting with her little red spade.

Her father, small and dark, sat back on his heels waiting
for her to finish. He was about thirty, handsome, self-
assured. 'I've been watching you all day,' he whispered to
Ann. 'I've been sunbathing up there all day.' He nodded
towards a strip of grass outside one of the nearest caravans.

'I saw you there,' Ann said.

The tide was coming in, a froth of water beginning to
trickle into the moat of the castle. It would soon be washed
away. Cleanly and decently rubbed out.

'I'm going to the pub later on,' he said. 'Do you feel like
joining me? Just for one drink? Just for . . .?' The look he
was giving her, the intensity of his voice were dangerously
familiar. She felt every cell of her body dying all over again.

'The White Lion in Llandre,' he said. 'Do you know it?'
He moved a fraction nearer to her.

'About eight,' he whispered. 'I'll be waiting for you.' He
picked up his daughter just as the first wave reached them.

'I have to go,' Ann said.

'Good-bye,' she called to the little girl, and without a
backward glance, left them and ran into the sea.

The sun was still blazing, the sea still warm and calm,
but she suddenly felt limp and exhausted; her shoulders
and her thighs ached.

She turned over on her back and lay like a piece of
driftwood, letting the small waves lift her. The sun burned
her closed eyelids.

'Free. Free as air,' she said aloud. But the words were
suddenly bitter in her mouth.

Myra's Mother Goes Gallivanting

It was a cold grey house, germs behind the curtains and in every cupboard, according to my mother, and children everywhere else, its smell neither pleasant nor unpleasant but distinctive; I'd recognize it even today.

I was allowed to play with Myra, the eldest child, but only Outside in the Fresh Air, Remember, and on no Account inside That House.

Myra's father was away in a sanatorium.

Sanatorium was an awesome word, though for me it had no exact picture.

Myra's mother sometimes went gallivanting.

I had an exact picture of gallivanting. It was to go into town on the four o'clock bus in a black coat with fur collar, hair tightly curled and a look of pale desperation.

When Myra's mother went gallivanting, she didn't come home till late, so never mind scholarship homework and piano practice, I had to go to keep Myra company.

When she came to call for me, my mother used to give her a drink of warm milk which she hated but drank, her blue eyes half closed over the top of the cup like someone drowning.

As soon as we got out, she used to spit on the garden path, wipe her mouth on her sleeve and shudder. Then we used to hurry to her house to give the little ones their tea, which was usually baked beans.

I was bigger than Myra though nearly a year younger and it was my task to wrestle with the big black tin-opener, the sort that unwillingly wrenched the top open, or almost open, one mean jagged bite at a time.

When the children were particularly hungry, which they almost always were, Myra didn't wait to heat the beans, but spread them cold on thick slices of bread, and though there was never enough for me – anyway I'd already had my tea which was nearly always something nasty like stew – I used to eat the leftovers at the end.

Baked beans was my favourite food. We didn't have them in our house.

When there were no tins of beans in the cupboard, nothing but baking powder and gravy browning and dripping, Myra fried things in a big black frying pan; slices of potatoes and cooking apples and carrots and swedes and anything else we could find. I finished off those leftovers too, though they sometimes gave me a stomach ache in the night.

After the meal, we threw the dregs of the sweet yellow tea – made with condensed milk, which was my second favourite food – into an enamel bowl for the cat and then put the cups straight back on the hooks in the scullery.

Then we took it in turns to do the ironing.

When Myra's mother went gallivanting, she left the washing – half dry and rather less than half clean – rolled up in bundles on the dresser, and it needed to be ironed because the little ones always had to have clean clothes the next day because nobody stopped them playing in the mud.

I wasn't much good at ironing, but then neither was Myra – nor her mother – and anyway the object was less to smooth the clothes than to dry them; one carried on until that precise moment when they stopped steaming and started changing colour.

Many of the dresses and jumpers had once been mine, but my mother had warned me against mentioning this, and I didn't, but I took special pride in ironing those. At home I was only allowed to iron tea cloths.

The little ones played outside if it wasn't raining too hard, but even after we'd finished the ironing, Myra and I usually stayed indoors; to show we were in charge, I suppose, and at ten and eleven, very nearly grown-up.

Sometimes we'd retire into the front room.

This was a large square room with pale mauve wallpaper and an ornate marble fireplace.

'I love this fireplace,' I used to say, patting it as though it was a horse.

'It's marble,' Myra would reply, 'I think it's worth quite a lot of money.'

There wasn't much else in the room that I could comment on.

Myra had told me that the sofa and chairs had been sent away to be re-covered in cherry red velvet and of course I always believed her.

'We'll be able to sit in here when the suite comes back,' she'd say. 'We'll make a big fire and sit in here.'

'I love the fireplace,' I'd say, 'and the wallpaper.'

The room smelt musty like the cupboard in the vestry where the hymn books were kept.

'We could have a party,' Myra would say. 'This room is big enough for a party, isn't it? Perhaps we'll have a party next Christmas when the three-piece suite is back.'

'Perhaps we could dance now,' I'd say. 'Do you think your mother would mind?'

We'd both stare at the carpet which was as threadbare as old sacking.

'I don't think so. Come on, let's do the waltz. You can lead.'

Myra would hum the tune, I'd hold her in the required manner and we'd dance sedately round and around the cold empty room.

After what seemed like the appropriate time, Myra

would stop humming, I'd bow, she'd curtsey and we'd go and stand by the fireplace again.

Then it was time for me to say, 'What a beautiful picture. Who is this beautiful woman with the beautiful baby?

'It's my mother and me,' Myra would say with just the right show of modesty. 'Didn't I tell you before? It was taken in a studio during a holiday we had in the Isle of Wight.'

I can still remember the love and pride in her voice as she said 'The Isle of Wight'.

I'd take it from the wall and examine it with unaffected amazement. Myra was so plump then, and robust; little dimpled cheeks and arms and the prettiest feet, round as little pincushions. And Myra's mother was a different person, soft and kind and carefree, the way a woman is, I suppose, before she has six more children and a husband in the sanatorium.

My eyes were misty as I fixed the picture back onto the nail over the fireplace, but Myra was always happy.

Only occasionally, on very fine evenings, would we be tempted out to play a game of hide-and-seek around the two sheds and the barn and the empty pigsty.

Cowboys and Indians was a less successful game. Myra and I chose sides as we did at school, but quite soon the three little ones on my side had defected to her, so that I was always a lone Indian, while she had a sizeable posse of cowboys at her command. And while everyone was ready to accept that only Indians could have war cries and bows and arrows, nobody could stop Jackie from being a horse and kicking out at my shins if he thought I was getting the better of Myra.

Once when we'd all been out together, we came back to find an old tramp standing by the back door. We'd been half-expecting him as long as we could remember, and now here he was; grey and sinister, bent as an old tree, eyes the colour of dirty rainwater.

We were all frightened, even Myra and I.

'Our mother is resting in bed,' Myra told him. How clever she was.

'We won't disturb her then,' the old tramp said. 'P'raps you big girls could fill my can with some nice strong tea and while you're doing it, I'll chop some firewood for your mother.'

We hurried to the kitchen and put the kettle back on the range.

'Oh look, he's got the axe,' I whispered, lifting my hands up to show Myra how they were shaking.

'He's not going to murder us,' she said firmly. 'There's too many of us for a start. And anyway there's nothing here for him to steal.'

She was right. All he did was to chop a bucketful of firewood and then come meekly to the door for his can of tea.

'I've given you two spoons of sugar,' Myra said as she handed it to him.

'Thank you Miss.' He turned to go.

But then Jackie came to the door, crying his eyes out. 'She's not in bed,' he said. 'Mama's not in bed. Why did you say she was in bed? She's not. She's down town again, that's where she is.'

'Ah, but she'll soon be back,' the old tramp said, seeming not to notice or care how he'd been deceived. 'And big boys don't cry.'

He turned to go then, waving to us from the gate.

'I'm not a big boy,' Jackie said, his fists in his eyes.

Myra picked him up and hugged him. He was only three, much too young to understand the way to deal with tramps.

Jackie, and Len who was four, often cried for their mother when they were tired or upset and sometimes Gwenno who was six, but very small, joined in.

Sometimes we played concerts to cheer them up.

Myra, her hands clenched tightly in front of her as though they were trying to run off somewhere, would sing in a wavering contralto voice – like Madame Glendora who'd once had a stage in the National – 'Oh, for the wings, for the wings of a dove. Far, far, far away would I roam.'

My song was about a farmyard. I didn't have Myra's acting ability, but I got almost as much applause because I went on longer.

Josie, seven, could do a ferocious squint and reel off twenty to thirty swear words like bloomin-old-cow, bum, crikey-heck, knickers and titties very fast. Myra laughed and clapped like the rest of us, but always warned him that he must never use the words outside the family. She was very concerned about their manners, warning the boys against pulling up girls' skirts or peeing against the wall in the playground and the girls against asking other children for the cores of their apples.

Then Glenys, eight, small, wiry and double-jointed, would do cartwheels and handstands. She was good at juggling too, but since we seldom managed to find even one ball, she wasn't able to demonstrate this talent. Sometimes she pulled out one of her front teeth instead.

By popular demand, the concert ended with Davy's impersonation of the Headmaster intoning the Lord's Prayer. Davy was Glenys's twin, but plump and fair while she was thin and dark. Though they looked so different, they were as close as two halves and could jabber away to each other in words no one else could understand. Miss Harris called it monkey-talk and got red in the face if they did it at school, but Myra and I thought it was extremely clever.

I'd noticed that neither Miss Harris, Miss Jenkins Infants or Mr Bowen the Headmaster smiled at Myra and the little ones in quite the same way as they smiled at children like me, who had clean clothes and tidy hair. Even in Sunday School, the teachers only gave them exasperated little half-smiles and asked them if they'd remembered their hankies. In Sunday School having a handkerchief seemed more important than being kind or learning a verse or answering a difficult question. Once Myra had answered a question meant for the grown-ups. I remember the lump I had in my throat when Mr Lloyd, the superintendent said, 'Da iawn, merch i.' I always liked Mr Lloyd after that even though he had hairs in his nose.

At about seven o'clock we put the little ones to bed. They didn't have to wash or clean their teeth, just dived into bed in their vests, scrambling right down under the hard grey blankets to get warm, and smelling like puppies.

Then Myra told them a story which always began, 'Once upon a time there was a big happy family.'

My last job was to take Jackie out the back again. He shared a bed with the twins and they woke and made a fuss if he wet the bed. 'Will you give me a kiss, Jackie?' I used to ask him when I'd brought him back. 'No thank you,' he'd say, wiping his mouth with the back of his hand.

I had to be home by eight.

Myra used to stand by the window of the front bedroom she shared with her mother to watch me as I set off down the road. It would be getting dark by that time, and as I turned round to wave, I would see her disembodied face; nothing but her white face and the grey house.

With any luck, her mother would be back on the half past nine.

The Day of the Funeral

As soon as I woke up I remembered, and the day settled on me like a pall.

I've run a nursery school for seventeen years now and on the whole I've enjoyed it, though of course some days are better than others. I've had my share of difficult children but I've liked them all – at least when they've gone home – there hasn't been one who's really got me down. Some children can't sit still even for a minute, some spill their orange juice every single morning, some daub paint on the walls, I've had one or two pee into my giant castor oil plant, but they all have moments when they redeem themselves. Matthew Leonard won't use a handkerchief, but when I tell a story he gets so excited I want to hug him. Ellie Marshall bullies the younger ones, but when we listen to music, she puts her thumb in her mouth and comes to lean against me. Selena Judd . . . well, I won't go on. Enough to say that I like children and feel gratified whenever they seem to like me.

Occasionally there has been a particularly bad day. A couple of years ago Andrew Brown fell off a slide in the park and broke his leg; his mother screamed at me when she heard he was in hospital, but came to cry on my shoulder later, and the next day sent me a dozen carnations.

Today, though, is going to be the worst day.

Nothing like this has ever happened before; Emily Cooper's mother died last week, she's being buried today, and I've got to have her while her father is at the funeral.

She's an only child, good, quiet and sensitive, and she

doted on her mother. How can I possibly cope with her for a whole day, from half past nine in the morning until four in the afternoon?

Well, I always keep to a fairly rigid timetable and I suppose sticking to this in as normal a way as possible will help me to get through.

First, we have something approximating to a number lesson, when we measure tables and boxes with pieces of coloured string, or find how many beakers we can fill from jugs of various sizes or how much sand or salt or flour it takes to balance a given brass weight. You probably did much the same in your first school.

This is followed by 'writing' and 'reading', i.e. copying out letters from flash-cards and arranging them with others to form patterns or even words.

'I've got "cat".' 'Well done, Annie. Look everybody, Annie's written "cat" on her board.' 'I've got "sod it"'.' 'Well done, Martin. Now see if you can do "cat" or "dog" or even "bad boy".'

Then it's time for orange juice and biscuits; health biscuits, two each. 'I don't like these healthy biscuits.' 'Yes you do, Matthew, they're lovely and crunchy. And please use your hankie, darling. It's in your pocket.'

Then, if at all possible, we go out into the garden or the park for a quick blow or a leisurely game, and then it's time for a story, followed by free activity; squirming on the floor and bashing each other for the boys and quarrelling over the pram or the Wendy House for the girls, which takes us to the lunch break.

In the afternoon we have music, dancing, painting and model-making.

I suddenly remember Araminta. She's a large china doll which was given to us a few years ago by a Miss Perkins who's now in her nineties. One of my mothers told me that the doll is very valuable; she has a French registration mark on the back of her neck, underneath her frizzy yellow curls, so I only bring her out on special occasions, when some little girl is running a temperature, for instance, and I can't contact her mother.

Well, I shall let Emily have Araminta all day today, no matter how jealous the others may be. Usually she's only to be quietly nursed, but Emily shall change her and bath her, even wash her probably unwashable hair, and if we manage to go to the park she shall take her with her in the pram.

Even as I'm planning all this, I realise how ridiculous and pathetic I'm being, trying to compensate a child who's lost her mother by giving her a rather ugly Victorian doll to play with.

What else can I do, though? I'm not a child psychologist, not even a trained teacher; not a trained anything. I don't know what else to do.

I didn't know Emily's mother very well, it was only very occasionally that she brought her daughter to school. She worked in the City. I sometimes used to see her passing on her way to the Underground: smartly dressed in clerical grey or black and carrying a briefcase. She didn't look like a career woman; she had soft, very fair hair, worn floppy and straight. Her face was plump and rather timid, she was the type you'd imagine dressed in petal pink ironing a shirt or peering into an oven. I probably liked her the better for that.

When Jeff, her husband, told me that she'd had to give up her job, I took it that they were having another child and I suppose my stupid face lit up or something because he laid a warning hand on my arm. 'Cancer,' he said.

I could hardly believe it.

'Are they sure?' I asked. 'She's so young.'

'Twenty-four,' he said. 'They're sure,' he said.

I took another deep breath. 'Ah, but the prognosis is so different these days,' I said. 'Radiotherapy and chemotherapy, I can never remember which one does what, but I know that about two thirds of cancer victims recover completely, now, don't they? What with cobalt treatment and laser beams and . . .'

'Three months,' he said.

He was so brave, even managing to smile at me before he left.

When he'd gone, I felt faint. As I've said, I hardly knew Emily's mother, but the thought of her death seemed like a hand crushing my heart. She was so young, her face hardly more lined than Emily's, her rather round eyes as blue and clear. To my surprise, an image of her naked body came to me, soft and fair-skinned and rounded like the Cranach Eve.

Cancer the crab.

'Cancer likes young flesh.' Where had I heard that? Horrible, horrible, all evening I could think of nothing but the fair young flesh of Emily's mother being consumed by that dark scuttling monster. Horrible and disgusting.

Emily's father, Jeff, is a pleasant out-of-work young actor. The first day he brought Emily to school, he looked far more upset than she did.

'She'll be fine as soon as you've gone,' I told him, leading him to the door.

'I won't know what to do till she gets back,' he said. He would have loved me to let him stay.

Even now, he turns to wave at Emily four or five times as he walks away down the path.

Poor Jeff. As far as I know, he never even has interviews or auditions, let alone work.

His hair is brown and curly and he usually wears a long shabby tweed coat. He'd make a good infants' teacher, he seems keenly interested in the fairly predictable lorries and monsters and tower blocks we make from egg cartons and cardboard boxes and toilet-roll holders. When he fetches Emily, he often hangs about lounging against the radiator and chatting, relishing any account of misbehaviour and minor insurrection. 'How was Ziggy today?' he asks me, Ziggy being a particular favourite since I told him about the very convincing sick-noises he makes whenever we start on music-and-movement. He's interested in little Amy Jones, too, who's got her own vocabulary, like 'fropp' – bad and 'koopey' – good, and Kelly Martin who suddenly comes out with what he calls 'a singing'.

'Listen, I've got a singing;
Mystery; mystery, snow and fall,
The wind is blowing, the sky will burst.'

I know he'd love me to offer him a cup of tea, but I'm careful not to start that. I'm always exhausted by four o'clock.

When he came to tell me that his wife was dead, I was almost relieved. I'd been to see her a few times, taking some of Emily's careful paintings with me; and the last time I went, I couldn't believe that anyone would want her to suffer any longer. Her face was grey and taut, she could hardly smile or turn her head to look at Emily's pictures. 'Thank you,' she said when I got up to leave and I felt she was thanking me for going so promptly rather than for calling to see her. That was almost a fortnight ago.

So when he told me she was dead, I suppose I must have muttered something about it being a release, perhaps a blessed release, because he became agitated and angry. 'It's not,' he said, 'no it's not. Sometimes we were very happy. Even this last week we've had times of being happy together, Emily lying on one side of her and me on the other, and she knowing we loved her. And the doctor said three months and it's only been two months and nine days. It's not fair. Oh, it's not fair.'

I gave him a brandy and let him cry until he became calm and quiet again.

That was when I promised I'd have Emily on the day of the funeral. I knew it wouldn't be right for her to have to go to Leatherhead where her mother's family lives, to a proper, old-fashioned burial in the graveyard. How could I have agreed to that?

To tell you the truth, I felt even more sorry for Emily than I did for Jeff.

Oh, I know he was sincere and whole-hearted in his grief. I knew he'd always remember his pretty young wife, perhaps as the love of his life. But I also knew that he'd fairly soon have other loves. He's so warm-hearted and affectionate. I'm old enough to be his mother, but the way he appreciates even my company shows his utter dependence on women. In the nicest possible way, he's a ladies' man. In a year's time, perhaps sooner, Jeff will have found someone else.

But Emily? How does a thoughtful, sensitive little girl of four years old accept a mother's loss? In Victorian times, she'd at least be told that they would meet again in Heaven. But now? What had her father told her? Only that her mother loved her and hoped she would not forget her.

And what can I say? I suppose I can talk about her father, how unhappy he is and how they must try to help each other. I can mention her Grandmother and Grandad. Perhaps I can find a story about a little girl who has a special relationship with her Granny. Perhaps some dark, stirring music will be more suitable, today, than our usual dancing music. I don't know. I'm not sure of anything. All I know is that I want the day to be over.

Jeff brought her soon after nine, sooner even than I was expecting her, thrust her at me and left with hardly a word. He was in a dark suit – I'd never seen him in a suit before – and his hair had been viciously pruned.

We watched him going out through the gate and walking away. He didn't turn to wave.

'Today, you're going to look after Araminta for me,' I said.

'Why?'

'I thought you might like to. Would you?'

'Yes, I think I would. Yes.'

I'd already reached the doll down from the top shelf of the toy cupboard and she lay on the hall table. Her face seemed particularly vacant. On the whole I prefer sulky cabbage-patch dolls.

'Her dress needs ironing,' Emily said.

'So it does. Take it off and I'll do it. Come through to the kitchen. The others won't be here for a few minutes.'

Even though I hadn't finished washing up the breakfast dishes, I set up my ironing board and very carefully ironed the long white dress.

'Thank you,' Emily said.

When the others came, she showed them her charge. 'I'm looking after Araminta. She's had her dress ironed. This is her best dress.'

I didn't try to persuade her to do any number-work; while we were arranging coloured counters to match the dots on domino cards, she kept herself busy dressing and undressing the doll, bringing out the toy iron and ironing board to iron shawls and blankets for her. She made her cakes and biscuits from plasticine, and after feeding her, she washed and brushed her hair, and quietly nursed her during the story about Lucy and her grandmother and during our break for music (Beethoven).

After lunch she was still as good and trouble-free. Once or twice she let one of the others borrow Araminta, but hovered over them until they returned her.

The day I'd dreaded was going unbelievably well.

'How has she been?' Julia Templeton's mother asked me when she and the other mothers arrived at three o'clock.

'Wonderfully good,' I said.

'I'd want Julia to scream and kick,' Faith Templeton said. 'Not just there queening it over the others because she's been allowed that stupid doll for the day.'

'Daddy will be here soon,' I told Emily when all the others had gone – I knew he was going to be a little late – 'Would you like to take Araminta home with you for the weekend?'

'No, thank you.'

'Are you sure?'

'Yes, I'm sure. I'll put her to bed in the Wendy House.'

She carried the doll upstairs to the playroom and was still there when her father arrived to fetch her.

'How has she been?'

'Fine. Very quiet, but no trouble at all. What was it like for you?'

He didn't reply except with a shrug of the shoulders. Emily arrived downstairs then, and for a long moment he held the little girl tightly in his arms.

'Come along, chick . . .' he said then. I watched them walking off together hand-in-hand.

'Queening it over the others just because she's been allowed Araminta for the day.' Faith Templeton's words knocked about in my head.

I couldn't pretend that I, too, wasn't surprised and . . . yes . . . disappointed. Much as I'd dreaded the day, I hadn't wanted it to be quite as easy. Emily is a good, amenable child, but I can't say I was happy about her being so unemotional and so placid on the day of her mother's funeral. I couldn't help remembering how Jeff had cried: *It's not fair. It's not fair.*

It was eight o'clock before I had the energy to clear the playroom that night.

Araminta wasn't in the cot in the Wendy House. She was lying in the middle of the floor, her face having been very thoroughly smashed in. With the ironing board, I think.

She was a valuable nineteenth-century doll of French origin, but I cried out with something very like delight.

Out of that wretched day, I felt that one thing at least had made some sort of sense.

The Rugby Match

It was 1976 and the day of the England-Wales match at Twickenham. My husband had been unable to get time off to take the children, so the boys had had to resign themselves to watching it on the television.

After lunch (early, so that they would miss none of the pre-match coverage), when one was listening to some rugby pundit on Radio 2 and the other reading out an account of the 1925 International from the *Western Mail*, I began to lecture them on their half-yearly school reports, which by chance they'd brought home only the previous day: if they could devote to their school work one-quarter of the energy they squandered on rugby, etc. etc.

Tom, the elder, fourteen, raised his head from the newspaper just long enough to say that he'd jolly well like to see my school reports before taking any stick about his, and Edward said, 'Hear, hear!' – though that may have been to the excitable man on the radio.

It was a half-hearted challenge, but I took it up. 'You shall see my reports,' I said. At the time I thought they were fairly accessible, tucked away neatly in the bottom drawer of the desk in the study. But after a long search, pins and needles developing in my right leg, I wondered about going on.

My reports had been pretty good – well, excellent, in fact – but I felt more and more that the boys would be completely unimpressed. 'Listen to this, Tom: "Her exceptionally high marks are the outcome of quiet determination and industrious application. Harold S.

Jarvis, M.A. (Headmaster): But you should see her steak and kidney pie!" ' Predictable schoolboy humour.

Just as I was giving up, I came across a small bundle of papers stuck in the very back of the drawer. The sort of innocuous assortment of documents, I thought, that every family manages to accumulate: solicitors' papers about the purchase of the last house but one; a year's guarantee on a lawn-mower bought in 1964; the odd insurance policy. I don't know what made me untie the tape round them; I knew my reports wouldn't be among them.

They weren't the papers I'd expected. These were much older, even older than my school reports: my father's Army pay book; some yellowing newspaper cuttings; half a dozen old airmail letters, which I didn't read, only turned over in my hand. (It was more than thirty years since my father was killed in Normandy. I hardly remembered him, but I still couldn't read those letters.) Among them, though, was a folded sheet of lined white paper which I did open, almost in spite of myself it seemed. The writing was old-fashioned, the ink faded so that I could only just make out the words.

There's no point in my quoting the letter in any detail. For one thing, it was written in Welsh, and, besides, it wasn't the words, simple enough in themselves, but the sequence of events following hard on the letter's arrival which evoked bitter memories, opened the floodgates which I always had tried, and usually managed, to keep securely shut. I was a small child again, about six, and it was a summer's day towards the end of the war.

The letter was from my grandmother.

I had wanted to read it. My mother usually allowed me to read the letters from her mother, but this time she refused, quite sharply, and shut it away in the top drawer of the dresser.

I felt cheated. I could understand joined-up writing, and my grandmother, Mamgu, wrote such nice things about me: how pretty I was getting; how glad she felt that I was so clever at school; how proud that I had won the recitation prize at the Eisteddfod – things like that.

'Why can't I read Mamgu's letter?' I asked over and over again that morning. It was probably a Saturday – I seem to remember long hours with nothing to do; and when my mother went down to the shop in the afternoon, I took it out of the drawer and read it.

It wasn't the same sort of letter as usual. The writing was smaller and more difficult to understand. I remember running my finger through the lines, looking for my name and not finding it. I felt ashamed then, thinking that my mother might have kept it from me lest I should be hurt at my grandmother's neglect. The last two lines were the only ones I managed to read; the baby was healthy enough, though Mali had nothing for it, not a stitch of clothing, and she hoped all was well with us.

I put it back. I knew my conscience would trouble me for the rest of the day and, to make matters worse, the letter hadn't been worth reading.

It wasn't until I was in bed that night that I thought about Mali. She was a maid at Hendre Court where my grandmother was housekeeper and cook, a large girl with dark eyes and dark curly hair. She was nice enough to me when I'd been on holiday there in the summer. (We had spent a week of my father's leave at Hendre Court, my grandmother being in charge while The Family was at the seaside in England.) And yet I didn't like her much. She laughed all the time, for one thing, and at things I didn't understand; and when I asked her to explain, all she did was laugh again. Also, I admired girls who had fair hair and blue eyes and small, trim waists. I much preferred

Nano, the other maid, though my grandmother said they were both silly girls and prayed I'd never have to go into service, though I thought it would be a lovely thing. She hoped I would get a scholarship and go to the County School and become a teacher. This was every mother's (and grandmother's) ambition for her daughter when I was a girl. Only one thing was grander than being a teacher – that was marrying a doctor.

And to think that I became a teacher *and* married a doctor; double honours. But by that time my grandmother was dead, my mother was dead, my father was dead, so it hardly counted at all. In bed, that night so long ago, I started to think about Mali's baby, and to wonder why she had no clothes for it. Had it come as such a surprise to her? Did babies come so suddenly, with no warning? Mary, I knew, had been warned by the Angel Gabriel; but ordinary girls like Mali, what about them? Didn't the district nurse tell them, though? I felt sure she came into it somewhere. But if you were in service at a place like Hendre Court, perhaps the district nurse was afraid to call. Only the gentry called; people like Lady Spencer-Hardiman, who had said my grandmother's preserve was the best she had ever tasted. Preserve was jam. (I had never seen, let alone met, Lady Spencer-Hardiman, but my grandmother talked of her so constantly that I'd extended my patronage towards her, praying for her every night. She came after family, friends and animals in my list, but before teachers, the minister and Mr Edwards the Shop.)

When my mother came up to kiss me goodnight, I was almost asleep and couldn't help asking her why it was that Mali had no clothes for the baby.

My mother didn't say a word, but I shall never be able to forget her look. She picked up the candle to take it downstairs, so that her face was illuminated. The look wasn't anger. It was more like fear.

'I'm sorry I read the letter,' I whispered. 'Only I didn't understand any of it but the last bit. There was nothing about me.' I started to cry.

My mother lowered the candle and bent to kiss me. 'Never mind,' she said. 'Never mind.'

I touched her hand. 'Didn't Mali know about the baby, then?'

'She pretended not to know, I daresay.'

'Why?'

'When a girl is in service, having a baby is a disgrace – it lets everybody down. Mamgu was blamed for not keeping an eye on her, and she had all the extra work as well. Oh, it's a bad business, indeed it is.'

On one level, this confused me even more. On another level, a subconscious level perhaps, it made sense. There are other things than poetry which can be intimated before they are understood.

'What did she do wrong?' I asked.

'Perhaps she was too friendly with the soldiers at Moelfre Camp,' my mother said bleakly.

'Shall we send her some baby-clothes? We've got lots of my old things, haven't we?'

Next morning I tackled my mother again.

'Oh, please let's sort out some of my baby-clothes for Mali,' I said.

My mother was far more curt than she had been the previous night. 'No,' she said. 'When I give them away, it'll be to someone more deserving.'

I think my disappointment was because I loved seeing the little knitted things, pink and white, the nighties, hand-sewn and embroidered, the cobwebby shawls, the tiny kid shoes, all in their layers of tissue paper – Mother growing sentimental over them: 'This little jacket was made by your Great-Aunt Hester and it came all the way from Canada.

Oh, the trouble I had with this blackberry stitch! Would you believe I sent to London for this pram suit? Saw it in Mrs Owen's magazine and nothing else would do.'

After all, I wasn't particularly fond of Mali.

'You are mean,' I said in a shrill voice. 'Oh, you are mean.'

I think it was seeing the hurt in my mother's eyes which made me continue. I was drunk with a sense of power. 'Daddy wouldn't be so mean if he was home. Daddy liked Mali.'

My mother continued to stare at me so that I was driven on to further indiscretions. 'He was with Mali all the time last summer when you were helping Mamgu with the bottling and the jams. He liked her ever such a lot. Everyone knew it.'

I can't have said anything that my mother hadn't suspected, but perhaps I made her face what she was trying to escape.

That night, she committed suicide.

Of course, I didn't know at the time that it wasn't an accident. Except that I did know. I didn't know the word suicide, but the idea was in my brain without form or name.

My grandmother gave up her job at Hendre Court and came to live at our house. Two months later, my father was killed in action. I was not quite seven.

I cried a great deal for my mother because we had been very close. I don't think I felt my father's death so deeply, though I pretended to, when people said I should be proud of him, how he had died for his country and so on. However, I loved my grandmother and she loved me, and I suppose that saved me from utter dejection.

In the first year at the County School, the way that Miss Rowlands, English, had studiously avoided my eye when the subject of suicide was being discussed had hardened the tremor of unease I'd always felt about the circumstances of my mother's death.

I tackled my grandmother about it. She sighed and told me that my mother had been at a difficult age; she was turned forty, apparently, when I was born – an age when a woman felt spent; one day I'd understand. Also, my father had been abroad for three and a half years with only a month's leave in all that time; that was difficult too – one day I'd understand. I wasn't to think my mother was in any way wicked, only very, very frightened. We both cried a little, I remember. But I didn't get morbid about it; I was eleven by that time and four years is a long time in a child's life.

I was sixteen and already in the Sixth when my grandmother died after a short illness. Because of my studious nature, I was given a County Grant to become a boarder at a local private school.

It was on a half-holiday, about a month after the old lady's funeral, that I came across the letter for the second time; my grandmother must have found it in the dresser drawer all those years before and kept it, perhaps intending me to see it at an appropriate time. On rereading it I understood, for the first time, the cause of my mother's suicide; realized for the first time how my childish taunts had exacerbated the situation. I remember walking back to the school in a daze.

I turned all my energies to study. I did my A-levels in one year instead of the usual two, and after the examinations had a nervous collapse and had to spend almost six weeks in the local hospital.

It was while in hospital that I conceived the idea of finding Mali. It seemed to me fairly certain that her child, who would now be ten, would be my half-brother or sister. I had worked out the dates. It was harvest-time when my parents and I had spent a week in Hendre Court. I could remember days spent in the cornfields, my father stripped to the waist, Mali (I could even remember her green dirndl skirt and white blouse) teasing him: 'Look how brown he is, like an old Red Indian!' Falling against him: 'Aren't you strong! Are they all like you in the Eighth Army? No wonder we beat the Eyties.' It was May when my mother had committed suicide. Within days, probably, of the baby's birth. It all worked out.

I had to find Mali.

When I got out of hospital, my only living relative, an elderly second cousin living in Llandudno, asked me to stay with her until I went to University, but I replied, rather grandly, that I'd been invited to Hendre Court.

Within a few days, I'd packed my bag and taken the bus the thirty-odd miles to the village of Garth Wen where the Big House was.

My plan was to call at the Court, explain who I was, say that my grandmother had died leaving one or two mementoes for her former colleague, Mali Richards, and could they please help me trace her.

I practised my speech in the bus and tried to decide whether to go to the front door or the back. I was nervous but quite resolved.

Near the bus-stop and immediately opposite the West Lodge was a square, red-brick house with a *Bed and Breakfast* sign in the window, and I called to ask for a night's accommodation.

The door was opened by Mali. I knew her at once, though she didn't recognize me.

Yes, she could put me up, certainly she could. Come upstairs and she'd show me the room.

It was a pretty little room overlooking the hills. It was extremely clean; and though everything was plain and simple, there was no sign of poverty about either the room or the house.

Would I want an evening meal?

Yes, if it wasn't too much trouble.

No trouble at all if I'd take pot luck with the family. One and six she charged, if that would be all right, and nine and six bed and breakfast.

That would be fine.

She stood at the door, a question in her glance.

'I'm studying Welsh History,' I said – it was true, – 'and I want to see the manuscripts at the Abbey.'

'Fancy,' she said. She closed the door and left me.

Then I looked out of the window and saw my half-sister.

It was an extraordinary moment, like stepping back into one's past. She was as like me, or as like the person I was when I was ten, as it was possible to be: small, delicate-looking, straight brown hair, large serious eyes. I couldn't see the colour of the eyes, but I knew they'd be dark brown with flecks of yellow like mine. I started to tremble.

She was sitting on a swing under a sycamore tree, not swinging but idly moving the stones at her feet. She wore a blue cotton frock, and her legs were long and thin, like mine.

Within minutes, another girl, younger, squat and curly-haired, ran up to her, tugged at her dress and took her out of the garden to join two boys who seemed to have found something at the edge of a little stream. The other three were exuberant and noisy; she seemed politely interested but quiet and still, rather grave. I realize that I'm trying to imply a sense of her superiority. I mean to: it seemed that way to me.

I wanted to cry. I wanted to rush out and claim her, that other self. I was sweating as I had done in the hospital, sweating and shivering. Something had to be done.

I found my way down to the kitchen. I tapped at the door. Something had to be said. 'Can you possibly be Mali Richards?' I began.

'I was Mali Richards, yes. Mali Jones now. Who are you then? Stop a minute, don't tell me. The little girl Vaughan, isn't it?'

'That's right.'

'Yes, I can see it now.' For a moment Mali was shaken too. 'Your father was killed in the war.'

'That's right. In 1944.'

Neither of us mentioned my mother.

'And Mrs Reynolds left the Court to go and look after you.'

'Yes. She's dead now, you know. She died last autumn.'

'Dear, dear, I am sorry. I hadn't heard that. I wonder if they know, up at the Court? Nice old thing she was, though her bark was quite fierce at times.'

'When did you get married, Mali?'

'Oh, years ago, girl. My eldest is turned ten. I've got four altogether, two of each. Will Jones I married. You remember Will Jones? The cowman. He still works at the Home Farm, mind – only manager he is now.' There was pride, or at least satisfaction, in her voice.

I didn't remember Will Jones. Not even when she got the wedding photograph from the parlour. He was a pleasant-looking man with a shiny face, big ears, a nervous smile.

'It's a lovely picture,' I said. Mali had a hat of feathers and carried sweet peas and a very large horseshoe.

'He's a good man,' she said. The way she said it made me realize she was telling me something important. 'Loves the children,' she said. 'All of them. Do anything for them, he will. I've been lucky. Up to now.'

I sat on in the kitchen, unable to say anything. I sat on while she scraped potatoes, washed lettuce, sliced some ham, cut a mound of thin bread and butter, laid the table.

All the time I looked at that wedding photograph till Will Jones seemed to be smiling at me to weaken my resolve.

'I think I'd better go back,' I said at last, putting the photograph down in the middle of the table with the tomatoes and the hard boiled eggs. It made the tea-table look like a shrine.

'Yes, that would be best,' Mali said.

She ran upstairs to get my bag.

'You'll get a bus at a quarter past five from the finger-post. It may be late because of the Mart, but it hadn't gone – I've been listening out for it.'

She kissed me at the door; a sudden impulse, it seemed.

So I was dismissed. As was right. My presence could only have uncovered old griefs much better forgotten.

I never saw my sister again. Where was she now? Now.

My husband was already back when I returned to the sitting room; he'd been called out to a first confinement, but I'd known the baby would be born before the match. He and the boys seemed three large strangers.

'Where did you get to, love?' my husband asked, without a glimmer of interest.

Before I could answer, someone had scored a try.

'Genius. Absolute flaming genius!' Tom shouted, hurling a cushion at the television and hitting the cheese plant. Edward made a dive for Tom, got him on the floor and pummelled his head. Tom grabbed Edward's ear, pulling and twisting it for all he was worth. They were both laughing like idiots.

My husband turned up the volume to savour the applause.

I burst into tears.

'Now you've upset your mother with your row. Apologize, do you hear, or I'll turn the damned thing off.' He turned the volume up a little higher.

'Sorry, Mum.'

'Sorry, Mum.'

My husband came to sit next to me and put his arm round me. 'Never mind the bloody reports,' he said.

His grip suddenly tightened round my shoulder, 'Now watch this kick.'

I looked at the three of them; their solidity, their aliveness, their moronic concentration.

Loving them, I wanted to join them. But that afternoon my ghosts were more potent: a soldier-farmer on leave from the fighting; a middle-aged woman with fear in her eyes; two small girls – sisters who had never met.

But if I cried throughout the match, no one noticed. And if my eyes were red afterwards, it was put down to the flush of victory: Wales 21, England 9.

Happy as Saturday Night

My Mum wakes me up at half nine on a Saturday because I has to go shopping for her. But I don't mind too much. As Janice says, you has to take the rough with the smooth, and the rest of Saturday is real smooth.

We lives on St Beuno's, a tough part of Cardiff about four miles from the centre. The food shops up here are terrible expensive. They says it's because they're always being vandalized and that, but if you asks me it's because they knows that mothers with lots of kids and no car will go to them whatever wicked prices they charge. Anyway I goes to Kwiksave and the market behind Tesco's for my Mum. She gives me twenty quid and a bit extra for a taxi home and I get her some great bargains. I finishes up with six or seven plastic bags which is why I need the taxi back. She's got three little ones and a new bloke and that's okay by me. She don't interfere with me and I don't interfere with her, and like I say, I don't begrudge the time I spends getting her shopping in.

I've got these good mates, see, and we has a great time on a Saturday. We works hard in the bleeding factory all week and it's all for Saturday night. Afternoons we might go to Goldees or Top Girl and try on some clothes and we like things that are sexy, real sexy I mean, we're not afraid of flaunting ourselves because we always sticks together, so we're always safe. My Mum tells me to get things from her club, but it's much cheaper where we goes and anyway by the time the catalogue stuff comes it's already past it. Last week I got a tight black satin dress and it looked like it had been painted on me with shiny gloss paint. That's the sort of thing we likes. And long glittery ear-rings and thick glittery eye shadow and pillar-box red lipstick, sticky as hot jam, that's the sort of thing we goes for.

We always sticks together. As soon as we've had our tea, we'll all be at Kim's house or Sian's – where there's no kids to bother us – and we has steaming hot bubble baths and then we does each other's hair, either blow-dry or tongs, with masses of volumizer and mousse. We goes in for Harlequin colour rinses too. I'm Titian Red this week and Kim's Raven Wing, and the others, shades of blonde; Ash, Strawberry and Honey. And we borrows each other's perfume sprays so we smells terrific, the lads at the bus stop can smell us coming before they sees us.

We aims for the half-nine which gets us into town around ten and first off we goes to the Four Bars for a couple of vodkas which really gets us in the mood. There's five of us altogether. Four of us was at school together, that's Ellie, Kim, Sian and me, we've been mates forever, and Janice is Ellie's big sister but she's ever so nice. She's twenty-one or two, but she acts like seventeen, she's really one of us now. She started coming out with us to keep an eye on Ellie because she's the youngest of us and a real dare-devil, and their mother ended up in one of them rest hospitals – you know – so Janice looks after Ellie, but not in a bossy way.

Janice has got a husband and a kiddie, but her bloke don't mind her coming out clubbing with us on a Saturday night, he says it keeps her young and frisky. And besides he goes out with the lads on a Friday night and darts on a Tuesday, so fair's fair, I say, though my Mum thinks he's some sort of super guy, some sort of a new man, she says, too good to be true. His name's Charlie. I don't know him very well. Ellie says he's great, but whenever she says it,

Kim and Sian say, 'Well, he fancies you, doesn't he, oh yes, two for the price of one.' But I don't listen because it's not the sort of thing I likes to think about because of Janice. The baby's about a year old and he's called Jake.

Anyway, this one Saturday, Charlie goes out shopping with Janice and buys her a new dress. We're all ever so pleased because she can't spend so much on clothes as us single girls because of the rent and that. It's a brilliant dress too, gooseberry green crushed velvet and so tight you can see her belly button as well as her nipples and the cleft in her bum, and she's got a nice tan from spending her lunch-times in the park with Jake – he goes to Happy Times Crèche but she has him out every lunch-time – and Kim got her some tattoo stickers for her shoulders, two bluebirds on one and a pink heart on the other, she looked terrific. We was all pretty lush that Saturday, but she was dead lush, I mean it.

Well, I suppose it's about half past eleven when we goes sauntering down to Roxanne's in Dominion Street, the vodka we'd had making us very happy, giggling at everything and whistling at these rugby fellas, big and stupid as tanks, still standing outside the rugby pubs with their pints.

The bouncers outside Roxanne's are ever so friendly. 'Go home, girls, and put some decent clothes on your backs,' they says when they sees us, but all in fun. After ten minutes or so in the Ladies, putting on fresh lipstick and hairspray and that, we goes in and starts dancing, the five of us together. Then this bloke comes up to Ellie and manages to lure her away, but he's from up our way and anyway we knows Janice will be keeping an eye on her.

About one, one thirty, there's this terrific dazzle of lights and an announcement: 'Hold on to your knickers, ladies, our stripper has arrived. And it's South Wales's answer to the Chippendales, it's our very own Mark Emmanuel from Abercrave.' There's some half-hearted clapping from the girls and some groaning from the fellas and then this very loud Fifties music and here he is, Mark Emmanuel himself, very cool, singing 'Blue Suede Shoes' and taking off his white jacket and his tie as though he's God's own gift.

And I suppose he has got something too, because I starts thinking about sex, how I'm always turned on by words like fuck and shag, but how I don't want to do anything about it just yet because I remember how everyone used to say I'd love it in Big School, but I really missed being in the Infants where all we done was play around with coloured paper and paste and that, and in Big School you had to start learning your letters and doing sums and teachers stopped being nice to you.

Well, I'm half-way through school by now, first year at Maesderw Road Comprehensive, when I suddenly sees that Mark Emmanuel is down to his G-string and all the girls but me shouting 'Off, off, off,' and all of a sudden he comes right over to where we're standing and he's asking Ellie to go out the front with him, what for I don't quite know, but I suppose I can guess.

Ellie's got such a baby face and that's what seems to turn fellas on more than anything. She's seventeen, like me and Kim and Sian, but she looks like a dressed-up twelve year old, the way she stands with her feet turned out, her eyes big and glistening and her top lip not quite covering her teeth. Kim says she looks just like the girls laying back on fur rugs in her Dad's porno magazines, but I swear she can't help it, it's just natural to her, that half timid, half come-on way of looking.

And then everyone's urging Ellie to go out the front where there's this circle of lights focusing on Mark Emmanuel, and at last, looking back rather proudly at us, she goes off with him and he tries to get her to pull his G-string off. Anyway, she hangs back and he thinks she's playing it clever to keep the tension up, but Janice isn't fooled and she goes out the front to get her away. And then Mark Emmanuel switches his attention to Janice, but she's not having any, she slaps his hand away, only not to hurt, and she pulls Ellie back to where we're standing, and he finishes his act on his own, shows us his thing, and we all squeal politely – like we're supposed to – and then he puts on one of these black silk kimonos and sings more smoochy songs and that's the end of that.

Only it's not, because Ellie wants to see him after. She says he told her to go round to his dressing room and she's mad keen to go, but Janice says she can't unless we all goes with her and she has to be satisfied with that.

He seems a bit surprised to see all five of us, but he takes it in good part and gives us a drink each in a paper cup – it tastes a bit dusty – and asks did we like his act and we all says yes, but it's not Ellie he's trying to make it with now, but Janice, staring into her eyes and begging for it.

'We must go,' she says, very firm, 'or we won't manage to get a taxi. It was nice meeting you, Mark.'

He gives us all a kiss as we leave, but at the last minute he makes a grab at Janice who's last out the door, and pulls her back. We can hear a scuffle and we don't know whether to go back in or not, but in no time at all she's out again, but looking wild, her eyes gushing over with tears and her gorgeous new dress all torn up the back.

'Just look at you,' Ellie says, as though it was Janice wanting to go round not her. 'Your new dress is ruined and serves you right.'

It's okay,' Kim says. 'It's only the seam and my Mum will run that up for you on her Singer.'

'It's not okay,' Janice says, and now she's crying real

hard. And Ellie marches off with the other two following her, so after a bit I goes with Janice to find the manager and we tells him she caught her dress on a nail and we don't like to go out like that. And he says not to worry, and he finds her a long white mac someone's left behind and then we has to go because by now everyone's gone, even the bouncers, and the manager wants to lock up.

There's no sign of the others when we gets out and we haven't got the money for a taxi because we always chips in one fifty each and no one would take Janice and me to St Beuno's for three pounds, which is all we've got left. (To tell you the truth the taxi drivers aren't any too happy taking all five of us, but we tells them we're all under eight stone, so it's only like taking two and a half big blokes and then they're generally okay.)

Anyway, there's nothing for it but to walk so we starts straight away. I've never liked bloody walking. Even in the country, even in daylight, even with some half-decent shoes on, it's dead boring if you ask me, but this is a nightmare, grey streets, a mean wind from the river and both of us miserable, me because the others couldn't be bothered to wait for us and Janice because of her torn dress and being late home. We hardly says a word to each other the whole way.

By the time we gets to my house I'm dying for my bed, but I haven't got the heart to let Janice walk the last half mile on her own. 'Look, I'll come with you,' I tells her. 'You're a good pal,' she says. 'You can sleep on the sofa and Charlie'll run you home in the van tomorrow.' 'Okay,' I says.

Their flat is four floors up and the smell in the passage makes you want to throw up, but I don't say anything, just drags myself up the endless stairs.

When we gets to the hallway we can hear the baby

grizzling and Janice says, 'Oh hell, I bet Charlie hasn't fed him. I'll have to do it. Will you have a cup of tea?'

I offers to make it and she says to excuse the mess because she didn't have time to wash up the tea things and she doesn't clean through till the Sunday. So she fetches the baby and gives him his bottle while I makes us cups of tea and hands one to her.

After his feed, Jake wakes up good and proper and wants to play, but neither of us has the energy so he plays with the beer cans Charlie's left around the floor and we just sits and watches him like two old biddies.

After about five minutes building up the cans and knocking them down again, Jake gets sleepy and Janice pops him back in his cot which is in the corner of the lounge and then she gets a tee-shirt for me to sleep in and a blanket and tucks me up on the sofa. 'I hope Ellie's okay,' she says to me last thing. 'Of course she is,' I tells her.

I'm drifting off to sleep when I hears this commotion from somewhere. At first I think it's someone in the next flat, but then I recognizes Janice's voice and she's crying and saying, 'I couldn't help it. It wasn't my fault. I couldn't help it,' and Charlie's shouting, calling her a slag and calling Ellie a slag and even calling her mother a slag. And then there's another sort of noise and Janice shouting, 'No. Please. No, no, no.' And I pulls the blanket right over my head because I knows exactly what's going on but I'm too frightened to get up and help her. I just have to lay there and listen to it, the thud, thud, thud, thud, thud, until it suddenly stops.

And then I can't get to sleep again. Suddenly I hates life. Sunday afternoon when I has to go and see my miserable old Gran and then getting up at seven on Monday and all the week and working at the sausage factory with all the smells you can't get used to. It all seems too much to bear.

I'm on the point of having a good howl when I feels Janice's hand on my shoulder. 'Can I squeeze in with you?' she says. And I moves right up against the wall and puts my arm around her, and after a while she stops crying and we gets nice and warm.

'It'll be okay next Saturday, won't it?' Janice says, still sniffing a bit.

'Course it will,' I tells her. 'Next Saturday's going to be bloody brilliant.'